THE LAST LANGUAGE

Also by Jennifer duBois

A Partial History of Lost Causes
Cartwheel
The Spectators

THE LAST LANGUAGE

a novel

Jennifer duBois

MILKWEED EDITIONS

Published 2023 by Milkweed Editions
Printed in Canada
Cover design by Mary Austin Speaker
Cover art by Chad Reynolds
Author photo by Justin Perry
23 24 25 26 27   5 4 3 2 1
First Edition

Names: DuBois, Jennifer, 1983- author.
Title: The last language : a novel / Jennifer duBois.
Description: First edition. | Minneapolis, Minnesota : Milkweed Editions, 2023. | Summary: "Provocative and profound in its exploration of what makes us human, The Last Language is the story of Angela's work using an experimental therapy with her nonspeaking patient, Sam, and their relationship that ensues"-- Provided by publisher.
Identifiers: LCCN 2022059608 (print) | LCCN 2022059609 (ebook) | ISBN 9781639551088 (hardcover) | ISBN 9781639551095 (ebook)
Subjects: LCSH: Speech therapist and patient--Fiction. | LCGFT: Psychological fiction. | Novels.
Classification: LCC PS3604.U258 L37 2023 (print) | LCC PS3604.U258 (ebook) | DDC 813/.6--dc23/eng/20221220
LC record available at https://lccn.loc.gov/2022059608
LC ebook record available at https://lccn.loc.gov/2022059609

Milkweed Editions is committed to ecological stewardship. We strive to align our book production practices with this principle, and to reduce the impact of our operations in the environment. We are a member of the Green Press Initiative, a nonprofit coalition of publishers, manufacturers, and authors working to protect the world's endangered forests and conserve natural resources. *The Last Language* was printed on acid-free 100% postconsumer-waste paper by Friesens Corporation.

Even stellar conjunctions can deceive.
But let us rejoice a short time to believe
The figure is a symbol. That's enough.
—RILKE, *Sonnets to Orpheus* (11)

THE LAST LANGUAGE

Part I

Chapter 1

I HAVE BEEN ASKED, I'm afraid, to explain myself.

Not by the court—they don't want to hear it. And not by you, since we understand each other, and anyway they won't let me write to you. They've assured me of this several times, even though I haven't asked. I am under no illusions. I see how it all looks. I saw it all along, and yet—here we are. I guess that's the part that's supposed to be interesting.

Nietzsche says we must cease to think if we refuse to do it in the prison house of language. This seems to imply we have an option. *Tell me a story about Zembla,* you used to say, or, *Tell me a story about Harvard. Tell me how you fell in love with language. Tell me how you fell in love with me.* You'd tell me your own stories from your reading, your dreams, your own imagination—you had a real saga about a fortune teller and an illusionist and their great love affair in nineteenth-century New York City. I think you might have turned into a novelist, if we'd been allowed to go on.

I can only hope that, in the long years ahead, your stories will sustain you. That it's a better quality of silence, this time around. My deepest fear is that it isn't—that I have woken you in your coffin only to leave you there, forever. And yes, I *do* know how this sounds—as though I imagine myself to have conjured you, raised you Lazarus-like into existence, when we both know quite the opposite is true.

What I really mean to say is that this is how it feels, sometimes: as though I have left you something worse than dead. If I have—oh please, my love, forgive me.

Oh please, my love, forgive me either way.

But the people demand a beginning! Here's one that casts me as an extremely sympathetic figure:

Two months after my husband died, I was kicked out of the Annual Linguistics and Philosophy of Language Conference. At the time, I was four months pregnant with my dead husband's child. I was subsequently asked to leave my graduate program, which had already put me $78,000 in debt. I then suffered a miscarriage—because of the stress, possibly, though in this version, we'll assert the link with certainty. My four-year-old daughter Josephine and I moved in with my mother in Medford, Massachusetts—not the nice part—and I began hunting for jobs. My daughter was named after Jo from *Little Women*. Has there ever been a person more courageous, more endearing, in misfortune?

The stated reason for my expulsion from the conference was insubordination—of which curiosity, as Vladimir Nabokov has noted, is the purest form. I was scheduled to be on a panel with Alec Tyruil, my intellectual rival and personal archnemesis, and may have become too heated in my remarks beforehand. Complaints were made—Tyruil being, in the tradition of all academics, simultaneously bellicose and extremely prone to personal offense—and afterward, I was called in for a conference with the department head.

"Angela," said Dr. Fitzwilliams, on the day of my ejection from the program. "Come in, come in."

He always seemed surprised to see me, though he'd been the one to schedule this meeting—it's more accurate to say I'd been summoned to it, via a stern yet cryptic email from his administrative assistant.

"Have a seat," said Fitzwilliams, gesturing ambiguously toward two roughly equidistant chairs. I spent some anxious moments trying to figure out which one he meant. "Just allow me a moment to finish up here."

He clicked three buttons on his computer in quick succession; I had the distinct impression he was finishing a game of Snood.

"Now," said Fitzwilliams, wheeling around and fixing me with his stricken gaze. "How are you, Angela? I mean, how are you really?"

He spoke as though he was a dear friend from whom I'd been concealing the true extent of my devastation.

"I've been better," I said.

"Yes," he said, and shook his head. "I was extremely sorry to hear about Peter."

I knew he was sorry. He had told me so already. Everyone had told me, over and over, so much and so often that after a while I began saying that *I* was sorry right back. Which I was, of course, obviously.

This time I just said, "Thank you."

"Your daughter? She's—" I could tell he was about to say "well." "She's—I mean, how is she?"

"Not great!" I said. "To be absolutely honest with you."

"No. Of course. Of course not."

I wondered if Dr. Fitzwilliams had kids, I mean *really* had kids. He did have pictures of two teenagers on his desk, but this was standard dean-of-department office decor and didn't necessarily mean anything.

"Your daughter must want her mother in a time like this," Fitzwilliams said.

"She wants her *father*," I said. As she reminded me nightly.

"Yes," said Fitzwilliams. "Well." One could sense his fingers wishing to click upon something. The Snood again, most likely. After a pause, he said, "I've been in consultation with Dr. Cartwright."

"Oh?" I said politely. Dr. Cartwright was supposed to be my mentor in navigating the perilous pre-dissertation labyrinth. Or my minotaur, as I more often thought of him.

"He and I are in agreement."

"Oh, yes?"

"We think that you should take a leave."

"What?" I said, sitting back in my chair. "What?"

It seemed for a moment that I actually couldn't hear him; I had a sinus infection, on top of everything else.

"A leave, Angela," he said. "You need to take one."

I pretended for a moment to think about why this could be.

"Oh, because of the *conference*?" I said. "Because I really don't think that merits—"

"We realize you've been through a lot." He was sounding very firm now. "Most people in your position would have taken some time off already."

What people are those? I wanted to ask. Were there other people around here who'd lost their thirty-one-year-old husbands eight weeks ago and hadn't missed a single class or assignment since? Who were currently, during this very meeting, still wearing an industrial-sized adult diaper, as the last remnants of a child—of a husband, of a life—bled slowly into the cotton? If so, I'd certainly like to meet those people! I bet we'd have a lot to talk about! Instead, I said, "I see."

"It's been an awkward fit here in some ways, Angela. I know your interests don't entirely align with the focus of the program—"

"I can realign them."

Fitzwilliams smiled, which frightened me obscurely.

"Well, you'll have time to do just that while you're on leave," he said. "Think about your dissertation. Think about what really excites you." He leaned forward, and I could see the thinning hair on the very top of his head. I wondered if he didn't know about it, or if he had the kind of wife who told him. "But mostly, Angela? Take a rest. A real rest. OK?"

I turned one ear toward him, then the other, in case this was all a matter of aural mechanics. I realize now it must have appeared as though I was shaking my head.

"But my loans," I said weakly.

"We'll get you a deferment," he said, looking relieved to be fielding such a concrete objection. He leaned back, then frowned into my file, which I saw had been open on his lap all along.

"The stipend, though, is another matter," he said. "You'll probably need to get a job."

*

I have lately been revisiting conceptual semantics. A tiresome compromise, I used to think—this idea of a few crude hardwired concepts (space and substance, causation and agency) giving rise to all we name and know. A vector for mealymouthed intellectualism and craven commercial ambition, the kind of pop-philosophy difference splitting that appeals to its audience only because it makes the real thinking look so hard.

But I am reexamining my assumptions these days—in this regard, at least, I am reformed! I am even reading some Pinker—I was surprised, though not all that surprised, to find him in the library here. Causality, he says, is assessed not only by pondering what would happen if things were otherwise. It is also about sensing an impetus that is transferred from an agent with a tendency toward motion to a weaker entity that would rather stay put. In this conception of causality, I am the passive object. It was the agency of Dr. Fitzwilliams acting upon my weaker self—and, if we zoom out farther, the devious treachery of one Alec Q. Tyruil acting upon Fitzwilliams! Because Fitzwilliams, I am certain, is one of those people who constitutionally prefers to stay put. And if he had, I might still be ensconced at Harvard—writing my heretical papers, alienating my excitable colleagues, doing nothing of consequence or anything of harm. I expect I'm supposed to say here that I wish, I wish so desperately, that it were so.

Let us change the subject.

*

The evening of my dismissal, I wept into my mother's lap—quietly, I hoped, since Josephine was sleeping. I'd been doing this a lot lately, and I sensed there was a small part of my mother that enjoyed having me back in her arms, even if she was sorry about the circumstances. She'd liked Peter. We both had.

Years ago, my mother had told me she'd often thought about how there was a last time you rocked your child, and you never got to know when it was. I thought about never rocking JoJo again—or rocking her again as an adult, which was worse—and began to cry harder. My mother turned up the music—to drown me out, I suppose. "The First Noel" was playing. Did I mention it was almost Christmas? Well, it was! It was also only twelve weeks after September 11. This was not a personal tragedy, no, but the hijackers did depart from Logan airport. Nobody ever talks about that.

"It's OK," my mother told me. Which is a great thing to say to someone as long as you never define what "it" is. Unclear antecedents being the fundamental basis of all compassion.

"What?" I said pitifully. "I still can't hear."

"I know," she said, and cupped my head until I wriggled away from her like a toddler. I went to the window. On the street below, a pack of kids in Pats gear and beanies were towing a little sled along the sidewalk. I couldn't for the life of me think where they might be going.

"I was talking to Alan the other day," my mother said from behind me.

"Uh-huh." My mother talked to Alan every day. My mother was a social worker—she'd spent her life in the prisons, trying to minister to the irredeemable. Alan was her oldest friend, a veteran of some of the same clinics.

"He knows about an opening," she said. "There's a sort of lab job."

"A lab?" I said.

"Well, more like a center."

I pressed my finger against the window. Before me, frost made delicate arborescent patterns on the glass.

"What sort of job?" I asked.

It was an experimental therapy, my mother told me, invented by speech pathologists. Facilitated communication, it was called. It involved a typewriter, somehow—my mother didn't know all the details—and was supposed to help nonverbal patients with motor impairments. People with cerebral palsy, profound autism accompanied by psychomotor problems, that sort of thing. The therapy was new and somewhat controversial, but there'd apparently been some promising results, which the lab was hoping to re-create.

I turned around. "Controversial how?" I asked.

"I don't know exactly." My mother waved her hands as though batting away a mosquito—a gesture she often made when I spoke in those days. "I guess they don't completely know if it works yet. Or how well."

I told her this wasn't exactly my line of experience. But

the job paid squat, my mother noted cheerfully, and there weren't exactly a lot of people with master's degrees in linguistics running around looking for lab work. (Or Center work, I supposed, whatever that was.) Also Alan knew the director; he could put in a good word. I had the distinct impression he had done so already.

"This therapy sounds like a Ouija board," I might have objected then. "It sounds like it might be made up entirely!" This is what people often say, once they've heard my story and have decided to be skeptics. But in other contexts, most people are agnostic, maybe a bit intrigued. This was my reaction, too—though in fact, I had more reason than most to be dubious. I was still trying to be a linguistic determinist back then. Linguistic determinism posits that language is the essential foundation of consciousness, the only mechanism by which human cognition can occur. In a way, this was a grim vision to commit to—our native language is the language of thought, that's it, the end—and entirely at odds with the optimistic premise of this therapy: if thinking *was* language, the linguistic determinist would argue, then there was nothing to discover within people who didn't have it already. Maybe it was the bleakness of this worldview that made the gig seem appealing—maybe I was starting to suspect, even then, that there was a whole lot more to the story.

But mostly, of course, I was desperate. And then, finally, very relieved.

I went to JoJo's room, half hoping she'd wake so I could rock her back to sleep. She did not. This was good. She'd loved her father terribly; half the time she woke up crying.

A four-year-old's grief is a savage thing. I didn't truly think she'd ever get over it, though I planned to spend my entire life telling her she would.

Armenian has a word, *karot*, for a strong sense of missing someone: there isn't really a counterpart in English.

But then—I might have a job. I whispered this into the room like a benediction. A job. A job that might help people, and, at the least, would not hurt them. This was something. This was a lot. It was such better luck than I'd had in so long, in fact, that it was almost hard to believe it could be true.

Chapter 2

I HAVE TRIED MANY times to recall the first day I met you—first for my own reasons, then later for the court's. Still, some of the details elude me. It was autumn—October 13, according to my testimony—and I think I can conjure a hint of incipient rain, of rubicund leaves and ashen sky. The feeling of a coming school year. That faint electric sense that somewhere very near, new lives were just beginning—very old ones starting over.

Rudeneja: the Lithuanian word for the start of autumn, as exhibited in nature.

I was probably scrambling along your sidewalk, my folders spilling from my bag; I probably—more than probably—was late. Josephine, I suppose, was with my mother. After some debate, I'd left the device in my car—I will confess I was a bit unsure of your street (you lived in a scrubby little neighborhood somewhat north of me), though not because it was so unlike my own. But there was its heft to consider, and the distance I'd parked from your house, and the implications of showing up at your door with my person not only disheveled—my hair being the sort that trends toward anarchy at a faster rate than the rest of the material universe—but also obscured, buried beneath a hunk of technology that resembled, in both appearance and attitude, an overgrown graphing calculator. This image suggested something like the exact opposite of the device's effects; I didn't want it to make a bad impression, either.

I'd spoken to your mother only once on the phone. She'd told me you lived at number twenty-one, "with the bright yellow shutters and Mary in the yard"—no article for this Mary, though there were several others on your street, and yours no grander than the rest. Your mother, however, was unmistakable: she was sitting in the doorway, smoking a cigarette and radiating the delicate ferocity of an ocelot.

"Sandi?" I said.

"Howdy." She was blonde and slight and somehow nicotine sunken. I could see this even from the driveway. "Guess you found the place."

She stood—to introduce herself, I imagined—but turned instead and went into the house. I took this as an invitation to follow. Perhaps that should have made me nervous—this tendency of your mother's to dispense with the formalities, to eschew the obvious, when so much of what I had to say to her was both. Though I'd done a lot of intake meetings at the Center, this was my first unaccompanied visit to a home.

I followed your mother through the doorway, down a dark-paneled hall and into a small yellow kitchen.

"Have a seat," she said, gesturing toward a clean little table with a green glass ashtray at its center. "You want a cup of coffee?"

"Always," I said. Your mother nodded. Your kitchen was neat, minimally decorated, with west-facing windows admitting a sooty, slightly melancholy light. The feeling of looking out from a train's second-class compartment: the sense of heading somewhere, but being nowhere in particular quite yet. There was a rickety-looking cuckoo clock on one wall, an Audubon Society wildlife calendar on another. October, disappointingly, was a ram; today's date had ANGELA written over it in big block letters, so evidently your mother did know my name.

"So I guess you want to hear the whole song and dance," your mother said, and handed me a cup of coffee. Her hands fluttered a little when they touched mine: a jittery optimism, I figured.

I took a sip. "What song and dance is that?" I said.

"Oh, you know. The whole disaster of my kid's life." Your mother leaned over and tapped her finger against my cup. "My daughter goes there, if you can believe it."

"Hm?"

I turned the mug around, revealing a logo from the University of Chicago. I admired it a moment, as though the mug was somehow the daughter's accomplishment, too.

"Oh yes," I said. "Terrific school."

"Pretty terrific," your mother said. Then: "Not *Harvard*."

She had mentioned Harvard a few times on the phone; she seemed to think the Center where I worked was *at* Harvard, and I'll admit I hadn't corrected this impression. It is fair to say I may have led your mother to believe my career was in something like ascendance—although really, for so long, and until so recently, it had been. How was I to know that my current professional divot was not a temporary blip, but the beginning of a terminal descent?

"You don't have to do a song and dance," I said. "I think I have the basic clinical picture."

"It sure ain't pretty," your mother said. "But I guess you've seen it all."

This was an overstatement by any measure.

"I've seen a lot of presentations," I said carefully. "And I've seen a lot of improvements."

"But now you're only gonna work with us?"

She'd brought this up on the phone, too. I'd told her the treatment was highly individuated; it took a while for clients to get used to the process, and, except in extraordinary circumstances, they stayed with a single therapist throughout their entire treatment. Your mother seemed to be waiting for a catch, so I'd added that I was a beginner too and only learning the process myself. This did not seem to satisfy her.

This time I just smiled and said, "I'm all yours. Well, yours and your kid's, I mean."

Using the word she'd used for you, of course, even though I knew that you were twenty-eight.

"Sam," your mother said, and smiled.

"Sam," I said. "That's a nice name." Although I'd known this too, of course, and in fact did not yet think it was really all that nice.

"You think so?" your mother said, and snorted. "It was his dumbfuck father's."

I blinked. At the Center, I'd made it a policy to always compliment the parents on their child's name—representing, as it did, one of the last uncoerced decisions they'd made about their child's life. Those parents, being rich, had had a lot more decisions than your mother: special diets, hyper-ritualized vitamin regimens, pricey homeopathic tinctures. Interventions commenced so early they seemed like a form of prophesy: all the stops pulled out at the first indication of nonadvanced development. The real snobs paid for private behavioral therapists—usually the last stop before some fancy residential school—and even the better public schools had music therapy. By the time those parents got to us, they were exhausted from all the choosing. They seemed relieved when I asked about their child's name, grateful when I said I liked it.

"Well," I said to your mother then. "It's your kid's name now."

"That's true," she said.

Sam. Later I would come to cherish it, with that fanatical adolescent devotion that finds a name in its anagrams, sees its letters illumed within other words. At the time it just reminded me of that egg-and-ham book Jo was always making me read. Dr. Seuss makes the same joke over and over—some seemingly anarchic figure ultimately proves benign—though that never seemed to bother Jo, my sweet uncorrupted child.

"So," I said, leaning toward your mother. "Tell me what you think I should know about Sam."

She raked her fingers through her hair, gathering a pile on top of her head, where she held onto it with both hands. It was not clear what she planned to do with it.

"Sammy and me," she said. "Well—we've always been best buds." She let her hair down all at once. "He was a really beautiful baby. I guess people always say that."

"Not always," I said. "They usually say 'advanced.'"

"Oh no, he wasn't advanced. Just normal. With talking, rolling over, all that. Well, he seemed normal to me, and nobody ever said he wasn't. I mean, what the hell did I know? I was eighteen." She reached into her pocket and produced a pack of Marlboros. "His dad was a creep, this was obvious to everyone, and I was still the last to know. Do you want a smoke?"

I shifted my weight. "No, thanks," I said.

"But Sammy was extremely pretty. People always told me he looked exactly like the Gerber baby. Had the dimples and everything."

Which people were those? It was never the right time to ask. Though you later came to seem to me quite beautiful, you never did have dimples.

"The problems started around eighteen months," your mother said, and fished a lighter from her other pocket. "Doesn't it always start around that time?"

"Often," I said.

She lit a second cigarette.

"He always liked my earrings, liked to pull on them and stuff. I'd say 'gentle, gentle,' and he'd laugh, like he knew it was a game. But he liked other things, too, back then. He had this crinkle book about the forest he thought was just hilarious."

I nodded. Josephine had had a book like that—it might have been the exact same one, actually—a few awkward verses about a bear and a fox, the meter puzzlingly askew. I didn't often think about Josephine when I was with my clients at the Center. Maybe it was the way those parents so often insisted that their babies did not start off like your average human infant—the kind that did nothing particularly miraculous, only communicated appropriately through wailing and spent many milky eons staring into your eyes.

"Anyway, one day he just only cared about the earrings," your mother said. "I mugged and clowned, did all this goofy shit—he would not crack a smile. It was like he couldn't even see my face. Before that, he had a really great sense of humor. He still does, actually. Doesn't go for the easy laugh, though. You should know that ahead of time."

At this, I began a laugh myself, then rescinded it, burying the whole thing beneath a glug of coffee that made me sound very much like a hamster. Your mother eyed me and ashed her cigarette.

"And then I noticed the—the movement stuff," she said.

"The psychomotor agitation?"

"Right. All of a sudden, he got real squirrely with his hands. And by the time I thought to worry about that, I couldn't remember how long I'd been trying not to worry about it. You know how sometimes your kid gets sick, and just when you're about to take them to the doctor, they get better, but then all of a sudden they're *really* sick, and by that point you have no idea if they're sick again or still?" I wobbled my head noncommittally. "I guess I just thought kids are weird. I had this nutty job with the T where I worked crazy hours. Dick Mullet—that's Sam Senior—was out of the picture again, just in time for me to turn out to be pregnant again. And all of a sudden I have this kid rocking like a

Romanian orphan. I mean not quite that bad, and not quite that quick, but, well."

"But this is what it felt like?"

Your mother ignored this and took a drag.

"All I know is by the time I took Sammy to the doctor, the guy was already mad at me. He'd been the nicest man, before. The way he talked to me then, you'd have thought I'd broken the kid's arm."

"That must have been really hard for you," I said.

At this, your mother rolled every single part of her body except her eyes: her shoulders, head, and torso all rotating backward in a totalistic gesture that managed to convey disdain without actually declaring it. It was a move that made itself completely legible, yet could never be complained about to a manager. I wondered how long she'd been practicing it.

"Oh, it was really just the frosting on my cupcake," she said. "Know what he did when he noticed I was pregnant?"

"No," I said in a smallish voice. I didn't want her to make that move again.

"This was a couple months later—I was really small back then, didn't show at all until the final quarter—anyway, the guy looks at my belly, looks at me, he goes, 'Perfect.' Like the whole thing was his problem, except it wasn't even really a problem, just some kind of inconvenience he had to cope with 'cuz I was a big dummy."

I knew a version of that look from my years in the service industry: the particular apoplexy of a person who imagines their minor annoyance is so morally significant it must have taken another person (me) many hours to personally contrive. But what your mother was describing was a much darker isotope of that, and it made me very sorry for her.

"And how did you respond to that?" I asked.

"I said, 'Yeah? Well your mom's the father,' and just walked right outta there. It was great because he actually had to think about it for a second. And this is a medical doctor! But I had to go back to the clinic in the end, because of the issues with insurance. They gave us a different guy, but God knows what went into our file."

"Well, there's nothing you can do about that," I said confidently. Having had some trouble with files myself, in the past.

"And then it was just, you know—zillions of drugs," she said. "All with names straight out of Scientology. All I can remember now is the Prozac and the Benadryl. And all these therapists named Katie. Physical, recreational, occupational. All Katies. You think that's weird?"

"Kind of."

"They wanted me to do all this craft stuff. You know, have him touch feathers, sand. I bought him a coconut once, who knows why. You know those things are really hard to eat?"

"I've never tried," I said. It was growing dark in the kitchen, I noticed; I wondered if your mother planned to turn on a light.

"I cut the tags off all his clothes," she said. She was speaking flatly now, as though bored with either the story or the audience. "I took him on these long car rides and let him shove his head out the window like a dog. When I was a kid, they made it sound like doing that would *instantly* decapitate you, but the Katies didn't seem too concerned." She took another drag, and her expression flickered slightly. "It's funny how your worries change, you know? Like when I first brought Sammy in, I was afraid they'd take him away somewhere. I really was—the pediatrician was that mad at me. And then it turns out there isn't any somewhere. I mean, not that I would have ever let them. Like I said, we're best buds. I just mean the state isn't exactly handing out a lot of help for cheap." She frowned and tapped her fingernail against the tablecloth. "Except for you, I guess."

It wasn't the state, in fact; it was the Center itself that would heavily subsidize our sessions, in the hopes of accruing the sort of data that would eventually attract government funding. But this seemed a minor distinction at the time.

"The lack of resources is so hard on families," I said instead. "This is exactly the gap our programming is trying to address."

Your mother was giving me a look like I wasn't quite the person she'd thought I was.

"Anyway," she said, "none of it made a difference. And no one seemed surprised when it didn't. Some of the physical stuff got worse, actually, and no one seemed surprised about that, either. I mean, he can walk, still, sorta. But it's a whole operation."

It was quite dim in the kitchen now, which made the outside look much lighter. I could see jack-o'-lanterns in the doorways across the street, awaiting their illuminations.

Your mother shrugged again. "I kept up with the language stuff the longest," she said. "We always had the radio on, you know. PBS, sometimes. This woman from church was coming to see him—I was going to church a lot back then—and she enrolled him in this 'book of the month' thing. But then I got that job at the call center, and started picking up some shifts at Shaw's, and I stopped going to church as much, and that lady sort of stopped coming. And Moira was a toddler by then—I mean a real toddler, always trying to kill herself. And she talked without me ever trying to teach her. So that's the story," she said abruptly, leaning back. "Like I said, I guess you've heard it all before."

"Some of it," I said.

Your mother stood and flipped a light switch. The kitchen flooded with chromium, and all the outdoor pumpkins disappeared.

"And?" she said.

"And I think it sounds like you've been a very good mother to Sam."

"Oh yeah?"

I took out my papers briskly then; something in your mother's eyes told me she was about to ask whether I had any children of my own.

"And I think that I can help," I said.

"Oh yeah?" your mother said again, and eyeballed the papers. "Can you teach him to spell 'hope'?"

That example was in all the pamphlets.

"How about 'Jeter sucks'?" she said. "'Fuck the Shart Weasel'? That's his father, obviously."

"When he learns to write, he'll write whatever he wants," I said. "I'm just there to help with stabilization."

"For the psychomotor agitation."

"The squirrely hands. That's right."

"And this is why it's free."

"It's why it's subsidized, yes."

"Because it might not work."

"Because it's new, and we're still learning. And also because, yes, it might not work."

We'd gone over all of this on the phone—the process, the possibilities, the tentatively promising results. We'd gone over the caveats, too: the newness of the technology, the many things that science had not yet reproduced. We usually saw improvements in a case like Sam's, I told her again now, but certainly not always. And we never knew ahead of time what kind or how much. These disclaimers, in particular, bore repeating. Because your mother, I could see, was a believer from the get-go. She was already staring at me with a dawning hope—tender and only half-concealed—and I sent up a silent little wish that I could help your family.

"Well," she said when I was done. "Nothing to lose, I suppose."

"Nothing to lose!" I said. But that wasn't true, and we both knew it. To gamble a hard-won hopelessness is to venture quite a lot; I could tell that she had ceded some of it to me already, and that it was already too late for me to ever give it back.

"All right," she said, and stood. "Let's go meet Sammy."

Chapter 3

I'D FIRST BECOME A linguistic determinist because I tried to study Russian. I'd been casually good at Romance languages in my youth, and at some point decided to make this a point of identity. And so I attempted the Slavs, and was quickly introduced to a hallucinatory landscape of semantic categories, metaphoric distinctions, rabbit-hole schematics—a kaleidoscope of nuance I struggled to perceive, let alone deploy. French and Spanish were like masks—sometimes crude, hardly ever convincing, but at least they fit your face. Russian seemed to occupy some different dimension altogether, and for the first time in my life, I felt not merely stupid but simple. English had bound my cognition within a maze of fairly narrow parameters; I might, with great effort, peek over the edges, but I would never live beyond them. I began wondering how far this might go.

And Harvard said: *As far as you let it*. I spent years committed to the idea of language as the fundamental infrastructure of thought, studying the way its particulars shape our every awareness—from our sense of direction to our conception of time, from our experience of smell to our subjective impression of whether or not a chair is a girl.

So it was bizarre—even perverse—that I found myself working at the Center only a few weeks after my ejection from the conference. The place looked like an underfunded daycare, and my being there at all further testified to the rickety state of things. I knew I'd been hired through a contemptible combination of nepotism, desperation, and bewildered credentialism, coasting in on the reputation of the very university that had not only dismissed me but left me functionally unemployable anywhere else. I was aware of being both under- and overqualified, in different ways, and hating all of them. I was also extremely grateful to have any job at all. It was almost an afterthought, then, that I didn't really believe in what the Center was doing.

The idea of the therapy was simple. The device was a sort of word processor, with common words preprogrammed; it was placed before a client, with a therapist beside him or sometimes behind—straddling him somewhat, like a cellist. The clients were nonspeaking and afflicted with various physical impediments that would make typing difficult; the idea was to mitigate these issues through nondirected physical support—to secure an atrophic elbow, to stabilize a tremor. I was dimly aware, even then, that the therapy had inspired some skepticism—quotidian objections about methodology and reproducibility, the purity of data, all that—and that the whole thing was a long way from FDA approval. My concerns, however, were higher-minded: you could not teach a person without language to tell you what they thought, I thought, because, without language, they never really had. In the years before I met you, I would have sworn—on a panel, in a court of law—that this was so.

But during my time at the Center, I saw many things I could not explain. How one client spelled "hope." (This happened right in front of me, while I was shadowing my supervisor, Leana, who later became quite famous.) How several clients—three at least—could identify colors without their therapist looking alongside them.

"Anecdotal evidence," according to the prosecution. But miracles, always, to the families. Your mother had gasped at the "hope" one, when I'd first spoken with her on the phone.

Most of the time, the results were less spectacular: the progress ambiguous, the language fragmented and prosaic. It was always a slow process, and awkward at first—sitting so close to someone, smelling the dense, soapy smell of their shampoo. (Kids' shampoo, always, even when the client wasn't a kid.) You'd work with a patient for hours only to get a hiccupy, rabbity lunging into something approaching a word—just enough to make you confident, never enough to make you sure. Sometimes the kid just didn't like you; that mattered but was always a hard problem to admit. This wasn't work for the tenure file—not clean and cold and perfect, like philosophy or linguistics—and the technology itself was not flawless. There were failures and embarrassments, too—like the savant who'd quoted Shakespeare but then, in a double-blind study, couldn't reproduce a single word—and even the decisive resurrections could be unromantic. One kid mostly wanted to tell his mother how much he'd always hated her ham sandwiches. But it didn't matter what they said: the mothers always cried. I cried about that one, too, later in the car—thinking of all those mother's sandwiches, all the misplaced care they'd meant, and how every not-ham sandwich of the future would be a way for her to say: you have spoken, I have heard you, you are known. Even if that child never said another word again.

The treatment didn't work for everyone—this I knew. And it never worked for anyone as well as it did for you. The day I arrived at your door, I was not expecting such profound transformation. But I did, by then, believe it was possible. Because by the time I met you, I was less certain than I'd ever been in my life. This made me feel tender and euphoric, as though I'd found a new religion.

After our conversation, your mother took me to meet you.

In the hallway outside your bedroom: an aquarium with bright neon fish flicking around testily; below them, a miniature scuba diver lolled beside an overflowing treasure trunk, dazed by his findings.

"My daughter's," your mother said. "I was promised they'd be dead by now."

She knocked on your door—shave and a haircut, two bits—but didn't wait for any sort of answer before she opened it.

What did I see the first time I saw you? I'm not going to pretend I saw you as anything like a man. My initial preoccupations were, it is true, strictly diagnostic. You were sitting in a wheelchair near the window, your features striped by the light through the blinds; when we entered, you moved your head in our direction without turning quite enough to actually see us. I'd thought you might be slight and light, but in fact you looked nothing like your mother: you had dark hair, a crooked nose, blue, somehow commanding eyes—I could see that even from an angle. Your fingers threaded the air before you, as though fitfully engaged in some kind of rosary. Your bed, I remember, was blue and neatly made, with a White Sox pennant pinned on the wall above it; in the corner, a mess of CDs teetered precariously beside a boom box. And certainly I noticed the books—rows and rows and rows of them, and not the ones you'd be expecting. In addition to *The Princess Bride* and *The Hobbit* and *Treasure Island*, there were Dostoevsky and George Eliot and Charles Dickens, as well as shelves of ostentatiously undergraduate political philosophy: Nozick, Rawls, et al. (Had your mother seen you reading *those*, I wondered? Maybe they belonged to your sister.) Your room smelled somehow wintry, I remember—a subtle crispness, not unpleasant—though I don't think it was actually any colder than the rest of your house.

A while later, we sat in your kitchen, the light falling silvery all around us. I sat beside you, not too close—as far away as I could be and still get at your hands; I must have been a little sweaty, still, from lugging the device from my car. Your mother watched as I removed it from its protective cloth. "It's a typewriter," she said, deflated, though I'd told her several times that this was more or less exactly what it was.

That first session was unremarkable: this according to my notes—later confiscated by the courts, then helpfully republished by the *Globe*. The goal was to familiarize you with the feel of the process: its choreography and proximity and lilt. I made a point of telling you every time I was going to touch you, then waiting a symbolic pause before I did—the therapeutic equivalent of your mother's little door-knocking routine. Clinically, the fact that you let me touch you at all was a step in the right direction, a fact I later recorded in my notes. Every time we touched, I felt a charge run through your body—a restless zinging just short of physical vibration. The psychomotor agitation, I figured. This could be worsened by anxiety or a sense of satisfying engagement with an activity; either way would make a regular word processor tricky, which was part of why you were a strong candidate for the treatment.

After a while, your mother produced a photo album; she wanted to show me your baby pictures. She spread them out on the table, chronicling your parabolic evolution: the banal acquisition of the typical competencies, then their miraculous vanishing. There you were: naked in a swimming pool in a season that's clearly fall. You being held by a tanned and mustached individual I could only assume was Dick Weasel; the awkwardness of the pose makes it clear this is an occasion. (He was appallingly handsome, your father, the kind of man who always gets a second chance or six.) Your mother stared at each photo intently—she was trying to chart your sinking, scouring the water for the precise point where the ocean had swallowed you up. But the photos admitted no revelation—only the stubborn fact of you, again and again. You playing a blue, soft-looking little guitar. You dancing to some music no one else can hear. You opening your mouth into a howl or a screech or a song or maybe, really, nothing: not some early sign of personality or pathology, just the random way your lips were shaped when a camera trapped you in a clue forever.

And then your hand jerked away from mine, and I snapped down into my chair. I hadn't realized how far I'd been leaning forward. I heard your mother say, "Oh, shit." It became apparent I had spilled my coffee—disastrously, theatrically, implicating many of my own materials.

"Oh, no," I said, as your mother frenzied toward the paper towels. And then: "I'm so sorry."

I was especially sorry a thing like this had happened on day *one*. I may have allowed myself a look of petulance while your mother's back was turned; it is possible I may have stuck out my tongue, which is an unfortunate stress reaction that I have. And then I caught your eye, and noticed you giving me one of the more sardonic looks I'd ever seen on a human face.

The cuckoo clock struck four, and I startled. God, I don't know how you live with that thing.

I looked at you again, and the expression was gone. Your mother was turning back toward us; the photos, thank Christ, were intact. We went back to looking at them, your mother and I, but something wasn't right this time. Looking at baby pictures was a common ritual with parents, and had never troubled me before. But now it felt like an intimacy I hadn't quite earned. I felt myself shifting back and forth in my chair—a little closer to you, a little farther away. I was having a hard time remembering exactly where I'd been before.

A new policy, then! I would not look at client baby photos, going forward. I did this a lot, in the beginning—made exceptions for you into general policies, then congratulated myself for my innovation. Those early days were a *parade* of logical fallacies—I think I'd ticked off every one by the time we really got started, and maybe even invented a few of my own. Some philosophy department should give me an award someday, assuming I ever get out of here.

Did I understand myself to have committed some transgression, in looking at your photos? I don't think so. In retrospect, I think my feeling was not one of trespass, but of debt—a sense that something vast was owed to you, something only I could give, and a promontory understanding that I would fail at this, was failing somehow already, in that dim little yellow kitchen with its weird geometries of light.

I decided not to put any of this in my notes.

Or maybe, I decided later that evening, it was just that I would have liked to ask your permission. I vowed I would one day.

And what were you going to do if I said no? you asked me much, much later.

"Beg forgiveness, I suppose."

And what if I said no to that?

I kissed you in reply. We both knew I'd never expected you to answer.

You pulled away and said, *I think forgiveness was your plan all along.*

Chapter 4

"How was it?" my mother asked, after my first day with your family. We were, as ever, eating spaghetti. On JoJo's plate, three winged horses were mauling a veggie meatball. (Did I mention we were vegetarians? Well, we were!)

"It was good," I said.

"Yeah?" my mother said. "What's the diagnosis?"

"PDD," I said. Physician Didn't Decide. I was in that phase of shallow expertise where acronyms were very exciting to me.

"JoJo, the ponies do not *like* spaghetti," said my mother.

"I think they do," Josephine responded shyly. One of the horses, a sort of glitzed-out Pegasus, had tomato sauce in its hair. I always enjoyed watching my daughter with her toys: that perky corvine intelligence that showed up long before language.

"Well, they certainly seem to be enjoying themselves!" I said.

My mother mouthed: *That is unhelpful.*

"It's autism, possibly," I said. "But it's not an entirely typical presentation." I was thinking of that look you'd given me. In those days I thought of eyes as stained glass windows without a church behind them. I suppose I still do—in spite of recent ambiguities, I still do not believe in a "soul" (no, not even yours, my darling). But there was a wild alertness in your gaze, and I'd noted this a beat before I'd registered the significance of my seeing it at all: you had a clinical aversion to eye contact, a fact I had recorded in my notes.

"He was very gifted as a toddler, apparently," I said.

My mother forked a meatball and said, "They always are."

"Apparently his mom has seen him reading."

"How do you *see* someone else reading?" my mother said. "Josephine, is that your way of asking to be excused?"

JoJo was wriggling in her chair with both her arms straight up.

"Yes," she said, and wriggled harder.

"Do you know a better way to ask?"

"May I please be excused, please?"

"One more bite," my mother said. "Then yes."

JoJo scrutinized her spaghetti, finally selecting a piece with very little sauce. I wondered if she didn't like it.

"There." She popped the noodle into her mouth and licked her lips hammily. "All done."

"All done," my mother agreed, and JoJo scooted off her chair and into the living room. Back to her little kitchen set, presumably.

A while later, my mother said: "You have some mail, by the way."

"Not a book, I hope."

"Well of course it's a *book*." She sounded a little hurt, though I didn't know why she would be. "But I thought you might be interested. It's from one of your old colleagues."

*

From Tyruil, of course, that old shit. It was his book, obviously, not that anyone asked for it. There was no note, no inscription, no request for comment. Only the stark fact of itself, with his dumb old face mugging all over the back and his dumb old name—ALEC Q. TYRUIL—prancing about in big block letters on the front. It was called *The Prism of Language: How Language Creates Thought*. The prism of language, good God. A pun on Nietzsche that absolutely nobody would ever get, except for the few people who did, who would swiftly die of self-congratulation.

I stared at the characters forming Tyruil's name: they were bright green and looked vaguely irradiated. On the back, a feeble blurb from Fitzwilliams; you could practically *hear* him not reading it. None of it came across as very academic. I suppose Tyruil was hoping to be some pop-linguistics breakthrough. Well, good for him. I hoped he was on NPR every day until he died. I hoped he had to listen to himself talk so much that he gave himself a stroke from sheer pedantry.

I had the impulse to throw the book out the window, but of course I did not. I have a reverential, nearly talismanic regard for books—all books, even Alec Q. Tyruil's. But that didn't mean I was going to read it. For one thing, I already knew what it said.

Take, for example, that look you'd given me. It was this—more than anything—that felt like the first pentimento of sentience: the word *water* etched into a palm. But Tyruil would argue—as I would once have argued—that this was impossible. Because language, in a very real sense, creates us. Not only generally, but down to the smallest particulars. Consider:

Russian has one word for "light blue" and another for "dark blue"; Russian speakers do not register these as variations of the same color. While the Herero of Namibia have the same word for blue and green; to them, this is a single hue.

Japanese numbers have different suffixes depending on what's being counted: little animals, things that are small and thin, etc. When asked to group items, Japanese children organize according to these categories. The literal-minded American child groups by shape.

Or take the Guugu Yimithirr of Australia, who don't have words for "left" or "right": they orient themselves exclusively in terms of cardinal direction. They are very, very good at this. Blindfold them and spin them around and move them to Antarctica. It doesn't matter. They still know.

The differences between our languages intimately shape who we become. But the absence of language was a different issue altogether. The absence of language was nothing like a foreign language, or a gestural language, or a string of undeciphered glyphs discovered in a cave. There was no feat of translation, no Rosetta Stone–like marvel that could retroactively create a sense of self-awareness in a mind that had not had it. Such a person would have subjectivity, of course—impressions, perceptions, preferences, in the way an animal or prelingual infant might. But the conscious mind must narrate itself into existence. It can do that in any language, but not in total silence.

If Tyruil was ever allowed to have an opinion about you, I knew exactly what he'd say. He'd say a person cannot conceive of what he cannot name. And *you* could not name anything. In a very real sense, there was no you. The person I'd seen looking out from behind your eyes wasn't really in there. He was certainly not making fun of me.

Our first few meetings were uneventful, and for this reason, I don't like to talk about them much. It seems disrespectful to tell a story about you that you're not even in yet—a story that, in those days, I was barely even following myself.

In those days, we sat in your kitchen. I evaluated your responsiveness and fine motor capacity, I guided you in the forming of letters and words. I explained and reexplained the processes and procedures; I tried, in my scripted little ways, to earn your trust.

"Forgive me," I would say. "I assume you know all of this."

Then I'd make you point at pictures: yellow sun, orange orange, blue fish.

There was often something noisy going on around us. Your mother liked to play the radio in the mornings—she seemed to know all the songs already; in the evenings, she'd put on television, although she never really watched it. She'd turn to almost anything—local news, *Friends*, *Letterman* when CBS wasn't coming in too snowy—and she seemed to have a special superstition about *Wheel of Fortune*. She used to make a whole big point of blasting *Sesame Street*, she told me later, until that got to seem too weird.

It was clear from the start you were a fairly promising candidate. You had a rangy, spasmodic physicality that was hard for you to control; fine motor stuff was, as your mother put it, "the real disaster." We spent a lot of those early meetings figuring out how our hands should go. Stabilization techniques vary between speakers: a thumb might be curled into a wrist, or an entire palm cupped within another; sometimes a clinician places a reassuring hand upon a shoulder, other times she is careful to avoid touching anything but the patient's communicating digit. This variation astounds some critics—those people who can only conceive of utility through militaristic repetition: NASA launches, routine elective surgeries, changings of the guard. But stabilization is like any other physical pattern two people fall into together—something like dancing, or breastfeeding, or kissing. A cadence that might be different if you were with someone else, but the entire point is that you're not.

I would have been the first to admit that there's a psychological aspect to all of this (although this is not an element I typically explain to parents—sounding, as it inevitably would, like a reproach). For many clients, the proximity to anything that feels like yet another assessment induces panic—the exact sort of frequency scrambling that makes it hard to select words—and contact with another body helps to create a useful sense of calm. But for others, I think, the fundamental reassurance is in the therapy's premise. Speech is not a key our patients must turn in order to be seen or believed or known; they are all those things already, we tell them through our touch, and words will come when they will.

Was this the way it worked for you? I never asked. We never spoke about the time before we spoke, once we could speak. It seemed a sort of courtesy between us.

In our third session, we moved up to your bedroom, where the angle of the light was better. (Lighting was always an issue: the device's screen was pretty dark, making it easy to misread things; the font, too, was unfortunate—a blocky all-caps lettering that made it impossible not to hear a sort of Stephen Hawking robot voice in your head.) I sat for long hours beside you in that little blue bedroom, studying your flickering intentionalities, your psychic telemetry. The current I'd felt the first time I touched you was there every time thereafter, though it surged at strange intervals; I spent eternities trying to map it. In the hallway, I'd watch a strip of sun creep along the carpet, eventually bisecting the aquarium's reflection, then moving off to somewhere else I couldn't see.

"How are things going in there?" your mother would ask from the doorway.

"Coming along!" I'd always say.

From the outside, I knew, the whole thing looked like nothing.

Nevertheless, we did make progress, eventually settling into a jumpy, flouncy technique, like a horse high-stepping in dressage. This seemed to discharge your restless energy some, though it did look extremely silly—I'd watched enough of it on video to know. It was standard protocol to record each session, sending tapes to the Center for review. Leana sent feedback: "Watch out you're not blocking his light (15:52). I don't think either of you noticed you almost spilled his soda (32:07). Is that a Sippy cup you're drinking out of (basically throughout)??" I was—your mother had given it to me, with much ceremony, on the occasion of my second visit. This, I suppose, was a joke; you'd jutted your chin and made an impatient whistling sound I later understood was a laugh. ("See?" your mother said. "I told you he has a great sense of humor.")

You never laughed again during these sessions, nor did I observe any expressions like that one the first day I met you—though it's true I was being judicious about eye contact, having so badly overdone it earlier.

Afterward, I'd sit in your kitchen, typing up my notes for the Center. I was very diligent, in those days, about all the documentation. Then your mother would offer me a cigarette, which I'd always decline. I didn't want her to know I smoked. Though she must have known already, it occurred to me much later, or she wouldn't have kept asking.

Chapter 5

OUR FIFTH MEETING, HOWEVER, was very different.

This was November 25, a Monday: I'd remember even if I wasn't legally obliged to. It had been two months since I'd come to you; fourteen since my husband had died. One year since I'd started my life all over, to see what I might be wrong about.

"I'm going to record this session," I announced, redundantly. I always did this, and I always said so. "I'm going to ask some questions, and we'll try to see if you can answer."

Exposition in dialogue: absolutely horrific. We'd gone over this a million times already.

"But this process can take a lot of practice!" On the tape, my voice is high and a little quivery. Girlish sounding, which my shameless lawyer thinks will help. "And if today doesn't work out, we can always try again."

On the tape, you can hear me shuffling papers, tapping on an object that has got to be your desk. And then the tapping stops. A car goes by, playing some empty-sounding music. I remember that you stilled to listen. And then I must have cupped your hand within my own.

"What's your name?" I asked you.

And then the music fades, and it is disappearing. And then I feel your hand move, with excruciating deliberation, beneath my own. It's surreal that this moment comes across as silence on the tape.

S, you wrote. Then very quickly, *A*. I was thinking that the proximity of these letters was unfortunate—the first might be a fluke, the second just a wobble—when your hand shot toward me, with a startling decisiveness, and landed on the *M*. Then there they were, *S*, *a*, *m*, all three letters right in a row.

I swallowed stickily—this part, you *can* hear on the tape. "And what is your last name, Sam?"

O'Keefe, you wrote. You included the apostrophe and everything.

"And how old are you, Sam O'Keefe?"

I am 28 years old, you wrote. When you could have just written "28."

"And where are we right now?"

I knew that these questions were inane, as though I was administering a lie test on a polygraph. But they were, of course, the protocol.

Medford, Massachusetts. Your fingers stuttered a little over the double *S*, but you made a point of going back to fix it.

"And how are you feeling right now, Sam?"

Bored and condescended to.

"What?" I pulled my hand away and looked at you. I wanted your face to tell me something about how to take what you'd just said, but you were inscrutable to me then. *A classic American deadpan*, you called yourself later—this was one of your many vanities.

"Well, I'm very sorry to hear that," I said. I was suddenly aware that I was sweating, and that I had been for a while; your mother, I figured, must really be cranking the heat.

"This *is* the standard protocol," I added.

You grimaced in a way that conveyed you realized this. I felt we were missing the point, somehow, burying the lede—you were talking, we were talking, you were fucking talking!—and I felt a little sour, I think, that you wanted to start with an argument. But then again: What did it matter? You had a personality, and this meant you had grievances.

On the tape, there's a pause where you can hear me fiddling with my notes. Absolutely nothing in that folder was going to tell me what to do next, but it seemed important that you not know that yet.

I put my hand back on yours. I'd forgotten to do that, unbelievably.

So, you wrote. *Can we talk about something interesting?*

Your index finger, I was becoming aware, was quite a bit longer than my own; your hands were rougher than they should be, as though you had some secret life in the world. Why was I noticing these things now? I didn't know. We'd been rehearsing this choreography for weeks.

"Sure," I said. Reflexively, I glanced down again at my notebook. The next part of our sequence involved me showing you flashcards with shapes of different colors, and maybe, if things were going very well, asking you to identify both. "So what interests you?" I said, and slammed the notebook shut.

Your hand began to move again, quite assuredly, in the direction of the middle keyboard. It sailed toward it, really, with a kind of boatlike surety: the sort of confidence that makes you ashamed for doubting, in your dark primeval heart, whether something quite so large can really float.

The White Sox, you wrote. I still remember the shape of it: the "White" like that just-launched vessel, or maybe an upended Pilgrim's hat; the "Sox" a spiky, intentional thing—some sharp little arrow, heading who knows where. But mostly I remember the glimmering movement of your middle forearm, the sudden legibility of your body. I didn't know what you'd say next. I only knew that somehow, I would understand.

Chekhov, you were writing. Then: *Ichthyology. That's the study of fish.*

"I know what it is," I said, though in fact I hadn't quite been sure. "Why the White Sox?"

It's as arbitrary as liking the team from where you're from, isn't it?

"I suppose."

You probably like the Red Sox, you said.

"I don't like any sports," I said. I never tired of declaring this.

But you are from around here.

I looked down and said, "Nearby." I was trying to keep my voice steady, even though of course you could feel that my hands were shaking.

I can hear it in your accent, you wrote.

"I don't have an accent."

You do. When you say "harbor."

"When have I ever said that?"

To my mother. The other day. You were talking about the outlets. You forget how much I've heard you talk.

There's a blindness that comes from believing you're

invisible. It wasn't that I'd forgotten. It was that I hadn't really known.

Plus no one likes the White Sox, you were saying. *Because everyone loves the Cubs. Because most people are total suckers for lost causes.*

"I think you might be one, too, if you like the White Sox just because nobody else does."

That doesn't make me a sucker, you said. *That makes me a contrarian.*

"Yes," I said. "I'm beginning to gather."

All of this, I should add, was going extremely slowly. Your typing was twitchy and tremory, involving a strange frenetic seizure of the upper arm. The letters appeared before us, peck by peck; between words, your fingers worried the air. Everything took forever in those days, though it's true it never felt that way, even then.

On the recording, another car whisks by; you can hear the sluicing sound of tires on slush outside the window.

I hope you don't think you're here to teach me to read, you wrote.

"No," I said.

Because, as you may have further gathered, I am excruciatingly literate.

"I'm not here to help you read," I said. "I'm here to help you talk. You know that."

But I can only talk to you?

I felt a bead of sweat forming at my temple. I abandoned your hand a moment in order to brush it away.

"You knew that part, too," I said. On the tape, I sound

like I'm reminding you of a set of terms you'd actually agreed to. If you'd pointed this out at the time, you might have been free of me forever.

If you want the truth, you wrote, *I haven't absolutely always been listening.*

I laughed at this, even though I felt, ludicrously, a bit insulted. I'd been stolidly diligent throughout our time together, absorbed utterly in my duties. This was a good thing. But I could see how it might look up close: graceless, literal minded. Devoid of those blessed destabilizing qualities, wit and imagination. I wanted to tell you there was more to me than that. That I could break a rule when it counted, and even sometimes when it didn't.

Instead, I said: "I'll be your only therapist, yes. And you'll be my only client. But only for a while, and only if you want us to keep going."

I was staring at your eyes again, I realized. I told myself my reasons were diagnostic—maybe therapeutic?—which might have been an early sign of some sloppy thinking on my part. Maybe this is when I should have left. Maybe this is when I should have turned and walked back down your driveway, with its crumbling angels and its frozen grass, dead but so brightly green that winter, leaving your mother to her kitchen and you to your own dark nowhere and me to my still darker nowhere deep inside your own.

Instead, I reached again for your hand. I believed that I'd believed in you all along. But then, nothing exposes doubt like revelation. And here, now, was the graceful length of your index finger, the inexplicable texture of your hands. I was feeling something opening inside me—something painful and permanent and deeply internal: an aortic rupture, maybe.

"But if you do, then yes," I said. "It will just be me for a while."

Well, you said after a time. *I guess it could be worse.*

Afterward, I went to your kitchen and poured myself a cup of water. I wanted to pour myself a scotch, just to be theatrical. I stared at the Audubon calendar on the wall. November was presided over by a grizzly bear, clutching a fish in its jaws and looking imperious. Somebody, I thought, should really change the month.

I settled for a second water, then a third. I tried to stand, then sat back down abruptly. I was shaking, I realized, and wondered how long I'd been letting that go on.

I wondered what I was going to tell your mother.

Chapter 6

I KNOW THAT YOU would argue with me about some of this account, if you could. Though what does "could" mean, in our case? You *could* not argue with me before I came to you, you *cannot* argue with me now; the dimensions of possibility have shifted, the reality remains the same.

But it isn't fair, you liked to say dramatically, with a look of parodic shock, whenever something very small went wrong.

The Tuyuca language requires speakers to specify how, or if, they know a thing is true. "I hear this is happening, I see this is happening, they say this is happening." Bulgarian has entire aspects devoted to the hedging of bets: the renarrative conveys information received through hearsay, the inferential covers statements gleaned from other facts, the dubitative expresses a sense of standing skepticism on the part of the speaker. I wish I could use these to tell this story—I wish I could acknowledge, with every word, that you have a story of your own. But I don't speak Bulgarian, and you can't speak at all now. So here we are.

We must imagine Sisyphus happy, you said once, after discovering green peppers on your pizza.

It's only lately, in retrospect, that these comments have come to seem funny to me.

But it isn't *fair?* No, it isn't! Which is why I'm the one telling this story.

*

Your mother sat across from me a while later, smoking and jiggling her knee. Outside, the sky was gray and somehow warm looking; it didn't feel as late in the year as it actually was.

"Sam had a real breakthrough today," I told your mother carefully.

"A breakthrough?" she said.

"We made some substantial—progress," I said, and swallowed. It seemed important not to let her know how stunned I was—and really, nothing about it should be stunning at all! Your breakthrough was wonderful, and surprising, and far beyond anything I'd expected to encounter personally. But it was also nothing more than we'd all believed was possible, all along.

"Progress," your mother repeated. The knee jiggling was starting to seem a bit compulsive. "What does that mean?"

"Well," I said. People always hear what they want to hear; the greater risk, always, is in overselling. "We had a conversation."

"Are you fucking with me?" your mother said. "I'm sorry."

"Not a long one, and not a—"

"Are you fucking with me? I'm sorry. But are you?"

"It's OK." I coveted her cigarette violently. "It's OK. And no, I'm not."

I tried venturing an explanation then, though what actually came out was something like the opposite—a collection of analogies and factoids, a couple of half-baked theories made permissible only by the sheer tentativeness with which they were advanced. This was exactly the sort of thing I used to do with my students on days I hadn't prepared: deliver a speech that told them that I was very smart, and that something very interesting was under discussion, and that even if I didn't know all the answers about that *particular* thing, I did know a lot of other things worth knowing. This often worked with undergraduates, where the goal is just to avoid boring everyone into mutiny. But your mother, I saw now, was really trying to understand me, and somewhere deep within my monologue, this sort of broke my heart.

"So, he's back?" she kept saying. And, once: "So he's in there?"

My answers, by this point, had descended into parable. For reasons beyond my understanding, I was talking about the Great Vowel Shift of fifteenth- to eighteenth-century English: a categorical paradigm inversion, but also just algebra—the crudest of code breaking, replacing this for that. Maybe that's what your breakthrough had been like, I was saying.

Or maybe that's what falling in love with you was like, I'd wonder later.

Or maybe none of it was like any of this, and similes fail me. I am not, after all, a literary person.

And so at last, I stopped talking. I took your mother's hand, so much softer than your own, and I told her, simply, that we had found the key.

She was looking at me in amazement.

"What did you talk about?" she asked.

"Fish," I said.

And then she finally burst into tears.

*

At the lab, I'd tried to unlearn the habit of mapping my old theories onto everything I saw.

Nevertheless, I was aware of how one might do it.

Language could still be the fundamental basis of thought if we assumed our patients had always had it: that they'd absorbed it, metabolized it, lived their inner lives silently within it, all along. In this conception, we were not teaching them anything, only granting them a means of expressing what they knew already. It's true the process didn't often look like this, when words emerged slow and fragmentary, with a relationship to the world that couldn't be completely arbitrary yet was never entirely reliable. But with you, of course, it was hard to imagine any other explanation.

Both theories did presume our results' validity (the results in your case, obviously, requiring the bigger presumption); in philosophy, we'd call them circular arguments. Except that they weren't arguments, just descriptions, and the context was not philosophy, only real human life. And certain inelegances were to be expected when you stepped outside of your own head and started trying to live in the world.

Live in the world, I told myself as I prepared for our second conversation. Also: *There's no need to get ahead of ourselves.* This is what I'd told your mother, too, when she asked if she might sit in on our next session. You and I needed more time to get comfortable with the technology, I told her; we needed space to develop a rapport. It was too early, our success too fragile, to scramble things with other variables. Soon, I told your mother, soon—and, happily, she seemed to understand this.

And so we were alone in your room again—which seemed a bit tidier, a bit brighter, since the last time I saw you. I wondered if you'd cleaned it, or if your mother had, and what either possibility might mean about your respective feelings—but then I reminded myself to cool it. *Live in the world, you pointy-headed ingrate. Live in the world right this instant!*

I'd made elaborate preparations for this session. I'd ditched the flash cards, arranging instead an array of prompts: postcards (Monet and Cezanne, cut from the MFA's spring catalogue); photographs from *National Geographic* (India in 1959 and Afghanistan in 1977; it seemed insensitive to show you places other people might actually go if they wanted); a black-and-white print of an interesting deep-sea fish. I'd brought along some texts as well: a short story—which I hoped you hadn't read—and that big *Globe* article about the priests—which I hoped you wouldn't care to discuss. These materials had seemed inspired to me while I was assembling them—so many leagues beyond the content I'd discussed with other clients, although there had been a Mozart freak who liked to watch *Amadeus* and cackle unsettlingly along with Tom Hulce. But now—sitting in your little blue bedroom, presenting these items to you one by one—they seemed insipid, underconfident, like ice breakers at a doomed party. You nodded appreciatively at the photos, declared Monet "corny," and paid some sustained, yet silent, attention to the fish. You perked up at the mention of Shirley Jackson but were disappointed to learn that the story was just "The Lottery"—you had that one in all your anthologies, though you told me you were curious about her novels. Then you started doing a weird pattern with periods and semicolons that it took me ten full minutes to realize was just a big black dot. At a loss, I let you keep going for a while after that.

For here, it seemed, were the possibilities:

You were absolutely, jaw-droppingly brilliant. We both were!

You were brilliant, and I was extraordinarily lucky. A witness to a miracle. At most, its unworthy messenger.

Nobody was brilliant and nothing was miraculous. You were just a very smart young man, ill-served by medicine, whose intelligence had been made legible by a clever yet simple therapeutic intervention.

Your hand began to move again, and I startled.

Amazed you into silence, I see.

I looked up, fixing my gaze just below your eyes. I was aware of feeling a little shy around you now. I wondered what unconscious habits you'd observed, in all those hours before I knew that you were watching.

"'Amazed' might be overstating it," I said. "I'm impressed, yes. I am pleased, absolutely."

Admit you're surprised, you said.

"I'm surprised," I said.

Admit you're shocked.

"I'm a pretty hard person to shock," I said. "Believe it or not."

Recursion, according to post-Chomskyan linguistics, is the fundamental basis of grammar. Sam knows that Angela is shocked; Angela realizes that Sam knows she is shocked; Angela pretends she does not realize that Sam knows that she is shocked—on and on, into infinite complexity and psychodrama.

So are you going to take me on the road with you? you were saying. *Demonstrate my gifts in circus tents, etc.?*

"Is that how our work together makes you feel?"

I'm joking. You talk like a therapist sometimes.

"Well, tone is a lot of subtext," I said.

I *am* your therapist, was the point I might have made.

I allowed myself a glance into your eyes then—just a small one, swift and shallow: a toe grazing a current, the rest of you safe on the shore.

"I was raised by a therapist, actually," I said.

That certainly explains a lot.

I had a feeling you were trying to bait me into asking you what you meant. I was already getting the impression that our way of communicating gave you, in certain key respects, the upper hand. You knew how I wanted to sound, which told you more about what I meant than anything I actually said; you heard the emotions I wished to project, and were probably catching echoes of a few I wanted to conceal. I had none of that on you. And then there was the way the last thing you'd said always blinked before me, like an impatiently tapping foot, goading me into filling certain silences I should not.

So no circus tents, you said after a moment.

"No tents."

But you are going to write about me?

"Maybe," I said. Then: "I guess a therapist would ask if that would bother you."

A normal person might ask that, too.

"Maybe you'll write about yourself one day."

Doubtful, you said.

"Why's that?"

I'm not a memoirist, you said. *I'm a fiction writer.*

"Oh? I've noticed the library."

Although it would have been pretty hard to miss. Besides your mother's self-help and positive-thinking tracts, there weren't a lot of books in your house.

I would hope, you said. *It's only here to impress women.*

"Your mother says you read them."

You never know when a woman might show up!

You gestured toward me like—*case in point.*

The collection, I remembered later, came from that subscription your mother mentioned—a kindly church lady had enrolled you in some book-of-the-month thing long ago and, for a time, came to read to you each week. After a while, she disappeared; the books, due to penance or dementia, kept coming. Your mother propped them up in front of you, you'd tell me later, always opened to random pages. By the time I met you, you'd read them all—many times over, though mostly out of order. It took you years to realize that *Frankenstein* has three narrators.

"So would it bother you?" I asked. "If I wrote about you someday?"

I guess it would depend on what you'd say.

My finger had slid into your palm on all the zigzagging around "depend"; I pulled it back.

"I guess that would depend on what happens," I said.

How about this, you said. *I do something interesting, and you write something nice.*

"Something interesting?" I said. Though surely you were aware you'd been more than interesting already. Exactly *how* interesting was a question I would struggle with mightily in the coming weeks. Part of the problem was that I liked your personality—I knew that even then—and I wondered how this might influence my characterization of your progress. Your language was confident and complex, yes—but was it dazzling? You had a sense of humor, sure—but were you, as an objective matter, a wit? I would puzzle over these questions well into the evenings, drafting and deleting entire reports.

At the very least, you wrote, *I will strive valiantly not to bore you.* You were writing with a syrupy slowness I would come to recognize as your lowest form of sarcasm, and that, I understood even then, meant you knew exactly what I was thinking, and that you couldn't bore me if you tried.

"Something interesting," I said again. I rapped my knuckle on the table, as though coming to a decision. "Yeah, OK. I guess that sounds like a deal."

*

All those books in your room: they'd made me sorry I wasn't more of a reader. That night, in my own bedroom, I found myself opening up *Pale Fire*.

I'd read this one before, actually, and remembered a bit about its tilt-a-whirl ontology, its Escher-esque structure (epic poem, unreliable narrator, footnotes). But for a failed language philosopher, what's most fascinating is Zemblan itself—a Germanic-Slavic hybrid that Nabokov himself invented. There might not be enough Zemblan in *Pale Fire* to say whether it comes with a completely imagined grammar—one imagines it does not—and yet there's something more than cleverness in the vocabulary we are given. *Nattdet*: "child of night." *Promnad vespert*: "evening walk." *Raghdirst*: "thirst for revenge." Any casual observer of European languages can see in these words a certain syncretic plausibility, suggesting some intriguing alternate history of the continent.

Had anyone ever tried to map it? I pondered this alone in my twin bed. Because Nabokov—I'd read just enough to know—actually did write with an eye toward clues, and tricks, and puzzles. Things that maybe we could figure out one day, if only we tried hard enough. And maybe we just hadn't yet.

And what if a lot of things were like that? I wondered as I fell asleep. What if *you* were like that, I permitted myself to consider—then laughed so loudly that my five-year-old came running in to shush me and remind me it was a school night.

Chapter 7

THE FIRST WEEK IN December, you said: *I have a confession to make.*

"Oh?" For a senseless moment, I was afraid you'd say you'd been faking—that you were a hoax, somehow. Although if you were a hoax, then you were my forgery, and nothing you could say should surprise me.

I researched you a bit.

"Oh?" I didn't understand how you might have done that, but then you'd done a lot of things I didn't understand. You had a tendency, even then, to offer up insights about me that I couldn't remember volunteering or betraying. In the beginning, before I'd seen the way she talked to you, I wondered if your sister had looked me up and told you things about me on the phone. Over the months, I would come to feel as though you might have somehow intuited my whole life story—first because I worried I might actually be as pitifully transparent as I felt, later because I hoped you knew me as deeply as I believed you did.

You're married, you wrote.

"Oh," I said. "Well, no."

I looked down at my hands. My wedding ring, obviously.

"I mean, I'm not anymore."

You turned your head to almost-look at me. I wondered if you'd turn it any further—you would do this, from time to time, though it clearly took considerable effort—and found I was relieved that you did not.

I'm sorry, you wrote.

"Yes," I said. "Thank you."

That probably seemed weird, just typed out like that, you wrote. *I'm sorry I don't have a way to actually sound sorry.*

"That's OK," I said. "Even verbal people don't get that feature automatically."

And a good thing, too: plausible deniability being the fundamental basis of all human sentiment.

Maybe we can come up with one? you said. *I'll tap S if I'm trying to sound sincere.*

"That will quickly lend itself to sarcasm," I said.

Is that so bad?

"I think maybe it's not great for now," I said carefully. "While I'm still trying to really understand you."

What if I don't want to be understood?

"Then remain obscure," I said. "I can't do any of this without you."

It was true. With your cooperation, we were beginning to develop a shorthand. If I guessed a word before you finished writing, I'd say it out loud and you'd hit Y for "yes." This made our exchanges go more quickly—approaching the pace of normal conversation, then seeming to accelerate beyond it. We had in-jokes, callbacks, little signifiers to indicate tone or something like it. When you were annoyed with me, you'd type very slowly, then even more slowly deny that's what you were doing. When I was annoyed, I'd find myself hewing ever more closely to the script—interrupting

things with drippy self-assessments, offering you education-
ally appropriate yet fundamentally idiotic materials I knew
you wouldn't ever want. I never went so far as to quiz you,
even though this was what I was supposed to be doing. Your
comprehension was an ironclad understanding between us,
and questioning it was a line we never crossed.

We were learning, I see now, how to fight with each
other.

So I hear you went to Harvard, you said the next time I
saw you.

"Oh?" I said.

My sources claim you're quite impressive.

"I didn't finish." I said this quickly, and for who knows
what reason. There was a strange, unsettling energy in the
room that day; even without touching you, I could feel the
restlessness of your body—something searching and cyclic,
zapping around with no outlet. In any case, one never acknowledges a compliment about Harvard.

So you're a dropout? you wrote. *Imagine me saying that in
a scandalized whisper.*

"Well, I didn't drop out, exactly."

You were kicked out? you wrote. *Imagine me falling into a
dead swoon.*

"Sort of," I said. Not for the first time, I wished we
weren't being recorded. "It was an intellectual disagreement.
I'm on a temporary leave."

How temporary?

"Undetermined."

How intellectual?

"Extremely."

And what was the nature of this disagreement?

I sighed. "It might be boring to you."

At this, you laughed. You had a lovely, multidimensional laugh, I'd noticed once I understood it: somehow rueful and generous all at once.

You said: *I don't think you understand the fundamental nature of boredom.*

And so I tried to tell you a bit—about my former neo-Whorfianism, and the idealistic instincts of its earlier practitioners—who, among other things, had wanted to demonstrate the sophistication of maligned groups through an investigation of their languages. And how its contemporary variant was, in some ways, a reaction to Chomsky . . .

Your eyes were widening in something I could only assume was terror.

"I mean, you asked!" I said.

I did. I'm just surprised you're answering.

"Why wouldn't I?" Though you were still, I could feel the energy coursing through you: it was the exact restlessness of someone who is absolutely dying to tap their foot, and the way they're not doing it is somehow more annoying than if they just went ahead and did.

You say you're trying to understand me, you wrote after a moment. *But what if I understand you first? Wouldn't that mess up your whole strategy?*

"There isn't really a strategy."

The handbook, or whatever? The extremely overwrought script you've been following?

I stood up then, and made a little lap around your room, pausing at your window. Winter, I realized abruptly, was extremely late in coming. It was weird it hadn't properly snowed, weird I hadn't noticed. On the street below us, a Star Market delivery truck was making a wide, inadvisable left turn.

I sat back down and turned off the recording.

"We reached the end of the script a while ago," I said. "It's all overwrought improv from here, I'm afraid."

My voice was hoarse, as though we'd been talking much longer than we had.

I thought you'd done this a bunch of times, you said.

"I have," I said. "I mean, under supervision. But it's never gotten this far before. I mean—what I mean is, it's never gone this well."

So I'm exceptional.

"Maybe," I said. Being of the opinion that exceptionalism is deadened by firm knowledge of itself. "Or it might be something else. Something we're doing that could be replicated." I shrugged, which I realized was a gesture one didn't see much outside of fiction. "Or maybe you're just really lucky."

That would be a first, you said, and I laughed a bit. You'd turned your head in my direction, but I was wary of meeting your eyes. I was aware of a jolt whenever this happened— intuitive static, I figured, the result of my strenuous efforts to anticipate your restlessness. Nevertheless, it was distracting; in my own mind, at least, it seemed to be accompanied by the sound of an air horn.

But so you're not trying to remain mysterious? you wrote. *And I'm not slowly chipping away at your reserve with my charm?*

I looked away.

"I think people always want to be understood a little more than they let on, and a little less than other people tend to manage," I said. "I think that this is probably what will happen with us."

Nah, you said after a moment. *Whole thing's a competition. Zero-sum game. I'm winning.*

"I don't think you actually think that."

What, am I being sarcastic? Even without an S key?

"I wouldn't presume," I said. "But I do think maybe you're forgetting how much is revealed in questions. And jokes. And in the things you don't say at all."

You leaned back and flicked your eyes toward me. A slantwise paper-cut-type glance: I felt it sting my face.

I think you're bluffing, you said.

"Maybe so," I said. "So here's a question for you, then."

Oh boy.

"Why ichthyology?"

I'd double-checked how to pronounce it.

Oh, isn't it obvious? you wrote. *Fish are beautiful and dumb and live in their own mute little kingdom.*

"You know you're very smart."

I meant dumb in the other sense.

"You are *far* too smart to be digging for compliments about your intelligence."

And yet no comment whatsoever on my beauty.

I laughed, and then again, a little harder. I was hoping to make my face turn red, I think—just in case it was, a little bit, already.

In academia, as in criminal law, one becomes aware of the case for the opposition.

Recursion, according to almost all post-Chomskyan linguistics, is the fundamental basis of language. And yet the Pirahã of the Amazon do not seem to have it.

To the linguistic determinists, evidential markers should attune speakers more intently to the sources of information. But in studies, Korean children prove no more skeptical than American ones.

The Jahai of Malaysia have an extraordinary scent vocabulary; in testing, they are far better than Americans at identifying smells. But it turns out that a nearby tribe of hunter-gatherers, speaking an unrelated language, are very good at this as well. The nearby rice farmers, speaking a similar dialect, are not.

Which raises the specter of cultural explanations. Arabic speakers are notoriously impatient with useless abstractions—"If all circles are blue and this triangle were a circle, what color would it be?"—and one can argue that this is a feature of their no-nonsense language. But the peasants of what is now Uzbekistan, quizzed in the 1930s, were exasperated by a similar line of questioning. "In the north where there is snow, all bears are white," they were told. "Novaya Zembla is in the far north, and there is snow there. What color are the bears?"

I do not know if Nabokov's Zembla is the same as the one in this question, although I like to imagine that it might be.

Either way, the subjects declined to speculate about the bears.

Your mother, of course, could not be held off forever. The second week of December, a public conversation was attempted.

This was always in the cards. The entire point of our work together was to generate some replicable data—this, as Leana kept reminding me, was why the Center was paying for it in the first place. Nevertheless, I'd tried to stall through underselling. "Soon!" I told your mother when she asked when she might speak with you herself. "Progress!" I told the Center when they asked how things were going. But Leana was already impressed. She'd sent me a gift basket after your first big breakthrough—believing, I believe, that my understatement was a form of professional-woman self-deprecation, and that I required bucking up by mentors. The fruit inside the basket was fancy and forbidding, the kind JoJo wouldn't touch. My mother pointedly said nothing about it; I assume she assumed it was somehow from Harvard, and that she was being superhumanly restrained. I let the whole thing rot on the counter.

At any rate, it was only a matter of time before you and I were deemed ready for a formal observation.

As was protocol, Leana would not be our observer; instead, the Center had sent a frank, trollish woman named Pauline. The day of her arrival, I found myself flitting around your room, messing with the setup. I checked the fall of light between the curtains; I plumped the pillows on your bed. This is where your mother would sit. For Pauline, we'd brought up a chair from the kitchen and set it in the corner, next to your CD pile. There wasn't really room for another.

I could hear your mother and Pauline murmuring below us in the kitchen, and I wondered what they were saying. I eyed your can of soda, then moved it a respectful distance away from the device. You gave me a look like *Are you nervous?* at the exact moment I shot you a jaunty glance saying *Don't be nervous!* We both laughed a little at that. *Sam knows that Angie knows that Sam knows that she is nervous.* If recursion *was* the fundamental basis of language, it was funny how much of it could happen in a silence.

And then they were coming up the stairs, and I could hear your mother's laughter on the landing. I found this confusing—Pauline not being given to witticisms, in my experience, and your mother not striking me as a suck-up—but I didn't have time to worry about it. Your mother knocked—shave and a haircut again—and I wondered if that little signature ever bugged you. I mean, really, who else could it be?

I opened the door, feeling the strange impulse to welcome your mother into a room in her own home. She caught the feeling and said, "*Love* what you've done with the place." Pauline gave me a nod—she had a wart on her chin with a hair growing straight out of it, which is not something I'd known existed outside of folklore—then folded herself up in her corner. I sat down at our table. Your mother retreated toward the bed, then stopped and hovered behind you.

"Hi, Sammy," she said brightly, and from her voice I could tell she had already lost her nerve.

"Well!" I said. "Are we all ready?"

Nobody replied. Pauline wasn't going to; that was her whole deal. I nudged you under the table and felt a semi-ironic staccato travel down your arm.

Y, you wrote, with satiric deliberation. Already, I felt, we were becoming coconspirators.

"Ready, Sandi?" I said. "You can sit down, you know."

"I know," she said.

But she didn't, quite, or at least not normally—hedging instead at the very edge of the bed, jostling her legs unsettlingly. I kept wishing she would either sit back all the way, or else move conclusively onto the floor.

I cleared my throat, which naturally sounded absurd. I had a little preamble prepared, but found I didn't have the strength for it. Instead I let my shoulder fall a bit, in a way that said I wanted you to take the lead, and exactly as I did this, your hand began to move.

I looked at your mother, who was staring openly. I'd stared at you like this all the time, until quite recently, but now it struck me as so obviously rude that I found myself looking away from her. In the corner, Pauline hunched unobtrusively, unmissably, over her notes.

Hi, mom, you were writing. *I like your haircut.*

Your mother sat back abruptly then, making a startled little "oh!" sound that turned into the beginning of a laugh; sometimes I think if she'd kept laughing, everything would have turned out differently. But instead she stopped herself—actually clapping her hand over her mouth, as though she'd said something insulting—and breathed, "Oh, Sammy." Her leg was jittering like a grand mal seizure; in the corner, your enormous pile of CDs threatened to fall over entirely. "Sammy," your mother said again. And then, *hélas*, she began to cry.

Your mother did not stop crying—not that first time, when she watched me speak to you, not the next two times, when she attempted it herself. She could hold herself together during the introductory small talk—you'd ask her about work or Moira, she'd ask if you remembered this or that detail from your past: some pet, some snowstorm, some song she'd played for you as a child. You would say yes, and sometimes no—though I got the sense your noes were conversational gambits, ways to give your mother the pleasure of reminding you of whatever it was she wanted to talk about. Sometimes she would ask what you'd learned that day, as one might ask a grade school student, and to this you'd offer strange little replies. *Today I swear I saw three different couples walking the exact same dog*, you'd say, or *Today I heard a radio segment about the secularization of Rumi*. Pauline's scribbling grew more or less frantic depending on your response; whatever the case, I could tell we had her attention. No matter what you said, your mother nodded with the same strange solemnity. She never asked about your reading or your thoughts, though this is not an uncommon dynamic in certain kinds of families.

She was understandably eager to attempt the process herself—and God help her, she did try. But whenever she touched you, she dissolved. She was eternally vexed by the question of how much weight she should be placing on your hand; she had a tendency to hold you much too limply, as though you were gravely wounded. ("Tell her she's not going to hurt him," Pauline would say to me later. "Tell her to let Sam show her how.") When your mother sat across from you, she watched your face so searchingly I half expected it to grow a new dimension, like a Magic Eye poster. ("Can you suggest she ask a little less from him?" Pauline said later. "As in, emotionally?" She was actually extremely kind, Pauline, although one tended to forget.) When your mother sat behind you, things inevitably devolved into a sort of clutching, almost rocking, often accompanied by some remark about the sweetness of your infancy. It was clear that those were the days she was missing; those were the times she would have liked to have back—and this seemed entirely the wrong spirit in which to try to properly acquaint oneself with a man of nearly thirty.

"It isn't working," said Pauline after the third attempt. "I'm going to suggest we take a pause."

"It isn't working," I told your mother later that afternoon.

We were standing in the kitchen, where it was always four o'clock: always darker than it should be, always earlier than it felt.

Your mother said, "No shit."

"I'm sorry," I said. "It's not your fault."

"Yeah?"

"It's a complicated technology—" I began.

"It's a typewriter," your mother said.

"And the emotions involved are—intense."

Your mother moved her head nonsemantically, or maybe I just couldn't see her very well. I don't know what it was with her and the lighting; I'd wondered if it had to do with cost, or if she had bad eyesight herself and didn't know it, or if the whole thing was some ritual of Catholic abnegation I hadn't heard of yet.

"The main emotion I am experiencing right now," your mother said, "is that I want to talk to my son."

The words were right, but there was something off about her voice—something too shiny and half-falsetto—and I think she knew I heard it. I flashed to an image of Josephine, stolidly anchoring the previous year's kindergarten production of some strange play about George Washington: all her lines delivered in the same ingratiating castrati timbre, with almost no awareness of what they meant.

"We don't have to do everything all at once," I said, and now I sounded shiny, too. "I don't think either of you are ready to talk quite yet."

Then I said your progress was extraordinary, just so your mom could say "No shit" again—which she did, a little reluctantly, as though this was becoming a catchphrase. She was crying again, I realized—with admirable restraint, holding herself quite still. But I could too easily imagine how it would sound up close, how her hot moist tearful breath might feel upon your neck. It was absolutely no way to have any kind of conversation.

"Soon," I told her. "Soon"—and she nodded so I would go away again.

Chapter 8

I WAS NATURALLY AWARE of the obvious objections. The big one in this case being: *Oh, really?*

The controversy surrounding the technology, according to my lawyer, must be both acknowledged and explained. This is precisely what he plans to do before the jury. He will remind them that people without speech are often capable of it with the right interventions—there are many documented cases where all that stood between a nonspeaking person and communication was a regular old typewriter. Also not in dispute is the existence of nonspeaking people for whom typewriters are not such easy matters: people with cerebral palsy, severe spatial impairments, etc. The theoretical utility of a therapy to help such people, he will point out, is entirely uncontroversial.

Nevertheless, nobody would deny that your progress, when initially considered, seems difficult to explain. You were not just speaking but speaking fluently, with a sophistication well beyond what many people who'd spoken all their lives could reliably summon. You had a perfect grasp not only of grammar and syntax, but of the uniquely social elements of language. You made jokes, even in our very first conversation; you occasionally—I would probably have admitted it myself—tried to flirt. Language wasn't just an abstraction that you'd mastered, which would have been remarkable enough. Instead, it seemed you'd been somehow using it—living in it, really—all your life. And this, one could be forgiven for assuming, was impossible.

But impossible—as my lawyer will point out—is a well-documented feature of conditions such as yours. The savant who can play a sonata perfectly after hearing it once, or tell you the day of the week for every date within a five-hundred-year span. These things are impossible, too, in the terms of any recognizably mortal cognition. More impossible, really, than the feat you'd pulled off—which, if we granted your supreme intelligence, could at least be explained in a legibly human story. You'd learned language the way everyone else does: by hearing it. Like many smart and enterprising children, you'd taught yourself to read. Through your reading, you'd internalized the nuances of social negotiation; you practiced the art of conversation by responding reflexively, silently, to whatever was being said around you. These thoughts—this secret language—was almost everything you had. All your time, all your passion and intelligence, went into its development.

(I tell the lawyer his whole defense is premised on linguistic determinism. He tells me to *please* not bring that up again.)

The prosecution's case, he'll tell the jury, relies on flawed reasoning. Much will be made, for example, of the therapy's unpredictable outcomes; and certainly, we will concede, its results do vary. But this makes sense when you consider that our clients are *definitionally* beyond assessments that rely on language or independent motor skills: anybody who had command of one or the other wouldn't be under this treatment at all. Results, accordingly, are extremely difficult to replicate. This doesn't mean they are not real.

(And my client—he will stress—had every reason to believe that they were real.)

But your particular combination of condition and capacity had never been documented before; what were the odds that I, a lowly ABD, dismissed from academia under shameful yet somehow boring circumstances, had discovered it in you? But here, once again, logic is at odds with intuition. I hadn't stumbled upon something no one else had noticed; I'd been given a tool that let me see something that had never before been visible. (And the training to use it—I'd studied the device for a year, my lawyer will remind the jury. If it seemed suspicious your overworked mother couldn't master the process in a month—as the prosecution will no doubt suggest it was—he'll invite them to consider how truly bizarre it would have been if she *had*.) At the end of the day, my lawyer will say, it was the device that made the discovery possible. In this regard, at least, I am entirely beside the point.

(I tell the lawyer he is good at catching logical fallacies. He laugh-scoffs and says yes, he knows that, thanks.)

And how rare a person had I found in you? We really had no idea. Your verbal gifts probably made you an outlier, yes. But how far out you lay—just beyond the edges, or off by some exponential margin, scrambling the whole system of scale—was impossible to guess. There might be millions like you, entirely capable of speech with the right technology, and we wouldn't know it yet. Because really, we'd only just begun looking.

*

Every day it got dark a little earlier, and every day I parked a little farther from your house. I found I didn't mind the walking. The houses had their Christmas lights up, and their funny little outdoor displays: twinkly reindeer in all the wrong numbers; the enormous glowing head of a sloshed-looking Santa; a Nativity scene in which the baby Jesus, upon inspection, turned out to be a baked potato. There were a couple of rotting pumpkins out still; one of them had tinsel on it. Poinsettias winked at me through windows when I hurried past them in the mornings; on the way back, I lingered, taking elaborate routes around small puddles. I picked out tiny things to tell you and wondered what things you might pick to tell me, if you could, and whether you would want to.

My car was always farther away, but it was always there. By the time I reached it, I'd lived many lives: I'd felt as generous as Santa and as twinkly as the reindeer, I'd felt the ludicrousness of the potato and the bathos of the pumpkin. My drives home took on the character of oral surgery; I'd regain sentience in front of my house, only hoping I'd had my lights on the whole way. "Are you OK?" my mother asked me once, and squeezed my hand in the way that meant she was thinking about Peter. Another time she wondered if I had a migraine, and another time she asked just what the *hell* was going on with me, here she was trying to read her newspaper and I was bouncing off the goddamn walls! Alan mouthed a question that must have been "Is she stoned?"

because my mother scoffed and loudly said she didn't think so, that dope didn't make a person act this way, and she (I) couldn't afford the drugs that did, and anyhow she (I) didn't even drink, although maybe this was the year for all of us to start.

"Maybe," I said mildly, infuriatingly, with the serenity of a novitiate.

"Jesus *Christ!*" my mother said and huffed into the kitchen.

Toward the end of December, I brought you a Chekhov story. I'd read it before, probably in college, though I couldn't remember it well and hadn't gotten as much out of it as I probably should have. In spite of my love of the Russian language, I had a sheepish sense I did not entirely understand its literature.

I'd made photocopies of the story, but you wanted me to read it out loud.

"Why?" I asked.

Your body spasmed in that way that meant a shrug.

I read all the time, you wrote. *I'm sick of the sound of my own voice in my head.*

"Why?" I said. "What does it sound like?"

You thought about it for a moment and said, *Tired. My voice sounds extremely tired. And anyway, I like yours.*

No one had ever said that to me before—but then, there were a lot of things no one had ever said. This was only just beginning to occur to me.

"All right," I said. "I can read it."

And so I did—stumbling a little over the names and antiquated language, my voice cracking a bit at the end, the part about colors for which there are no names in human speech. Afterward, we sat there and looked at each other. I felt kind of dumbly euphoric for no reason whatsoever.

That shift to present tense, you said. *When Gusev dies?*

"Oh, yes," I said. "Brilliant literary device." Though in fact I hadn't noticed as I was reading.

It's like a shift into this cosmic, eternal, out-of-time sort of voice, you said. And then: *It's like where I live.*

"What do you mean?" I said. I had wanted so badly to ask. So badly, in fact, that it always seemed obvious I shouldn't. And yet, on some level, you must have wanted me to—I was recognizing this, finally. Because you could not say anything by accident; you couldn't even pretend to. Here was an advantage I had on you, I realized with some tenderness.

Oh, you know, you said. *Out of time. Out of language. Falling down deep into the ocean, probably about to get eaten by a shark.*

I stared at you. You were looking so different to me now. It wasn't that you were suddenly becoming handsome; you'd always had a lovely face—symmetrical features, striking eyes, the whole deal. I'd even said so to your mother, long before it would have occurred to me not to. ("I know," she'd said sadly, in a tone that meant she got this all the time.) What was happening now had nothing to do with beauty; it was something much stranger, more substantial. Your features were assembling into new meaning, as foreign phonemes alchemize into words. It was hard not to keep staring—to keep checking, again and again, on this interesting process.

"I won't let you," I said, in a voice too high to be my own. I couldn't quite tell how much we were joking.

Oh yeah? you said. *You gonna fight the shark or what?*

So we were definitely joking. About what, I think we hadn't yet decided.

"I'd fight the shark, absolutely," I said. Somehow our breaths had gotten synchronized, which was weird; I held mine to get us out of sync, which was even weirder, and made me sound a little hyperventilic when I spoke. "I'd punch it in the goddamned nose."

Your gaze remained oblique, aimed at my forehead or maybe the door; the angle was the same and yet somehow felt different, as though it now contained the possibility of turning. As though the tilt itself was no longer a given, but a question. And as though I might, at any moment, find myself staring straight into your eyes.

What color were those eyes, exactly? I never thought to name it. It belonged to your eyes only; it did not somehow live beyond them; I would see it nowhere else.

Yeah, you said, after a whole long while. *I think maybe you would.*

Later, as I was walking out your door, your mother said, "Hey, Angie."

She was sitting on the porch, smoking a cigarette; I'll admit I almost tripped right over her.

"Jesus Christ," I said.

She was wearing a thin white bathrobe; her nose, I saw, was very pink. "Maybe I should take Sammy to a concert?" she said. "We used to do that all the time."

"That's a great idea!" I said, mystified.

I took a step toward the driveway, but your mother said again, "Hey, Angie." I turned. She was looking up at me with reddish, white-rat eyes; she had that kind of delicate face that varied wildly in attractiveness depending on what color it was. "Hey, Angie," she said. "You should come to Christmas."

I stared at her. I had no idea what she meant by this offer. I could feel a great Nixonian paranoia descending upon me; I tried to shake it off, giving an actual shudder your mother must have mistaken for a chill.

"Thanks," I said quietly. "Maybe I will."

Chapter 9

IT'S SPRING NOW HERE—AGAIN, and finally. It's strange to miss it, after slogging through another Boston winter. I served my time out there, like everyone else. Injustice turns out to be comprised of a million smaller injustices—I'm living in a pointillist absurdity, each day discovering a new dot.

A few days before Christmas, my mother said: "I don't like how hard you're working." I felt my expression seize a little, though my mother didn't seem to notice.

"I make six bucks an hour," I told her.

My mother said, "Exactly."

"I *need* the hours, is what I'm saying."

"Well, maybe you should take on another client."

"It's full-time work with *one* client," I said. "I've told you that a million times. It takes three months for them to get used to how you *sit*."

Although not in your case, obviously.

My mother sniffed. "I just don't think you owe those people your evenings."

I looked around the room. My mother was knitting some kind of garment, no doubt for some kind of needy individual; Josephine was twirling around behind her, wearing a bright green jumper. *Jeopardy!* was on, and one could only assume that Alan was on the way.

"It isn't like my regular evenings are so thrilling," I said.

"No," my mother said. "This is because you have a child."

"That's really only the half of it."

"You know she has a half day on Wednesday."

"She *does*?"

"Angela, it's her winter vacation."

"I *know* that." Josephine had taken a break from twirling and was now issuing instructions to her bear about what sorts of behavior would be likely to earn the approval or ire of Santa. I lowered my voice a bit. "I guess she'll probably want more ponies?"

"This 'hard'-to-forget 1964 chart-topper opens with a G7 suspended fourth chord," said Alex Trebek from the television.

"'A Hard Day's Night,'" my mother said serenely, and I looked at her.

She shrugged. "I mean, what else could it be?"

"OK," I said. "I'll take Wednesday afternoon off. Just tell me what I should do with her."

My mother bit off a thread.

"I told her you'd take her into the city."

"Not the Children's Museum, I hope."

"I didn't specify," my mother said. "But we haven't been downtown in a while."

"The marathon," I said, though I knew that had been the year before.

Josephine, having judged her bear irredeemable, had resumed the twirling. That green jumper she had on—I was fairly sure I'd worn it myself as a child. My mother must have squirrelled it away for a quarter of a century, in anticipation of this very moment. I was overcome by the ludicrous tenderness of this, the nearly sinister foresight.

"You're coming, too?" I asked her, defeated.

"I'm coming, too."

"All right," I said, and sighed. "We'll go to the aquarium."

On Wednesday afternoon, the three of us walked through the twinkling North End, all the way to the harbor. Harbor, I thought, harbor. Is there anything more odious than a Boston accent?

JoJo had briefly mourned the Children's Museum but was distracted by the prospect of a shark.

"A shark lives in the aquarium!" she'd declared to a group of BU students on the Red Line. One of them rewarded her by looking a little alarmed.

The advertised sharks were all crappy little dogfish, but Josephine was nevertheless amazed: to a child of a certain age, every damn thing is a wonder. We watched blue-tipped angelfish hover in their tank, a task-oriented ray looping around and around near the top. In the corner, glowing cuboids displayed deep-sea lobsters, like luminescent relics. I had been to Budapest once, for a conference, and seen some rotting saint's alleged digit in a church. The signs directing the way to him had pointing cartoon fingers, which seemed like a real missed opportunity. That was the only time I'd ever left the country. I knew better than to say any of this to Jo.

We saw leafy sea dragons and common cuttlefish and

spry little African penguins. We watched floating pumpkin-colored lanterns that turned out to be called sea nettles, and we stared into the empty, postpartum eyes of a balloon-fish. Then we rounded a corner and came upon an octopus: dome-headed and luridly bright, arranged somewhat messily in the corner.

"Now, Jo," I said, and stopped her. "These are really interesting."

"Hm." My daughter wrinkled her nose at me.

"No," I said. "The thing is, they're extremely smart. They can watch other octopuses open things and then figure out how to do it themselves." I thought for a moment. "One time, there was an octopus who got loose every night and went to eat other fish in the laboratory."

JoJo sprang back.

"Not this one," I clarified.

"But he could," she said.

"I don't think he'd do that while everyone's looking, do you?"

"I don't know," she said, regarding the octopus. "He might."

Actually, I agreed with her. His deep magenta color suggested a certain shamelessness.

"They can communicate electronically," I said. "They can see with their fingers in the dark." I knew some of this was not strictly true. "Their blood is made from copper and they have eyeballs that evolved completely differently from our own." I put my hand right up to the glass, even though there was probably a sign somewhere saying not to. "I think that other octopus was in Seattle."

"He's ugly," my daughter declared, with uncharacteristic confidence. "His feet look like the underneath of the bath mat."

"They do!" I said. "It's sort of the same idea, really—"

"*What?*" Jo shrieked, and my mother announced it was time to go see the seals.

I stayed behind for a while, communing with the octopus. He was from Alaska, apparently; his paper said he was already five years old. Exactly my daughter's age! And then I whispered aloud to him: "They say the best is yet ahead."

At the gift store, I bought Josephine an enormous bottlenose dolphin, even though we hadn't seen any dolphins and she had truly nowhere, nowhere, to put it.

Outside, afterward, we headed toward the water.

I was walking beside my mother; JoJo and her dolphin were running out ahead. I was thinking about your eyes again, and how their color was like the ocean's—not because they were the same, but because they both were singular and nameless. The ancients, in the time before dye, did not experience colors as abstract qualities separable from objects; their chromatic vocabulary, accordingly, barely extends past black and white. Thus Homer's wine-dark sea and oxen, his violet sheep and iron. Not mysteries of translation, or the past's inscrutable soul—just the things that Homer saw in the words he had to name them.

"'And what if one of the gods does wreck me out on the wine-dark sea?'" I half-shouted at my mother. "They used to think Homer was blind because he described the water that way."

"I thought they thought he was blind because that poet guy was blind?" my mother said. "In *The Odyssey?*"

"That, too," I said. "Obviously."

I'd forgotten that part.

Ahead of us, Jo was jumping in a puddle, the dolphin flopping helplessly beside her.

"You might have saved that thing for Christmas," my mother said. "If you really had to get it in the first place. How much did that thing cost you, anyway?"

"Oh, give us a break," I said. "I mean, really. What harm does it do?"

We had reached the water, somehow. Out beyond us, the waves were choppy and hypomanic; the sky above was white and sleek. It looked like it knew something I did not. I was, all of a sudden, in a very good mood.

"Cowabunga!" JoJo shrieked, splashing mud on her companion.

"I mean, look at her," I said to my mother. "I mean, she's just so happy."

I wound up spending Christmas Eve with your family. In retrospect, I do feel bad about this part.

"But it's Christmas Eve," my mother pointed out, when I told her where I was going.

"I'll be back in time for her bath," I said. JoJo's bath times needed careful chaperoning now, as she'd recently developed a fear of the bath mat. "And for the stockings, obviously."

Though in the end I wasn't, quite. I am absolutely sure

my mother put Jo to bed a little early, in order to teach me a lesson. You'd think I'd be angrier about that now than I was then, but really, it's the other way around. It hurts to think how much my mother must regret it.

And so I spent the evening singing carols with your family. Your sister was off building houses with Habitat for Humanity, so it was just the three of us: your mother and you, with me translating beside you. The device sat before us on the coffee table. You wore a floppy red elf hat and mugged every time your mother put a camera in front of your face, which was often. She'd been doing this a lot in recent weeks. I'd worried things might feel different between your mother and me, after the abortive attempts with the technology, and was relieved to find that she seemed genuinely content with our time as a trio. Your presence was an obvious fact to her, I imagined, and an obvious gift—perhaps it wouldn't have occurred to her to complain about the details.

And so that night we all watched *Rudolph*, and you ranted about its anti-feminist politics, and your mother told you not to be such a bad sport. I'd helped you order her a pair of earrings, the first gift she'd ever got from you. She cooed over them ecstatically. For me, she'd bought a scarf, surprisingly nice; I liked it almost as much as I'd been planning on pretending to. We gave you presents, too—from me, a gift card to an independent bookstore that had just started doing online orders; from her, a new pair of headphones. *These are awesome, Mom!*, you said—which didn't sound like you, exactly, though I reminded myself that I only knew one of your voices. Code-switching: the practice of alternating between two or more varieties of language in a conversation. It made me dizzy, to think of all I had still to learn about you, the many versions of you I'd yet to meet. You with your sister. You with friends. You at school—your mother and I had discussed this some—and maybe college, too, though she was less certain about that part. You on the bus, you at a coffee shop. You sailing across the street at the tail end of a Walk light, going somewhere that was only your own business.

Afterward, your mother said she didn't know if it was having you back or having me there, but either way it had been the least lonely Christmas she'd had in a while. I told her I felt the same way, and she gave me a sad little smile. It was possible she knew about my husband. I didn't think I'd ever mentioned Josephine.

I helped you walk me out—you in your elf hat, your goofy sweater. Your mother had strung some mistletoe above the door, and for half a second I thought you were going to get cute with me. And then I'd have had to say something like "Don't get cute with me" and you'd have had to give me a look like *I would never!*

But as it happened, none of this happened. Instead, you only squeezed my shoulder. Something was going on behind your eyes, though, something I hadn't seen before. I didn't know what it was, or how to name it.

I only knew that it was there, even if I could not.

*

The guy who found the people without recursion—he actually came up with an alternative.

Language, he said, is a matter of symbols in sequence. Recursion, accordingly, is entirely beside the point.

The sequence he proposed goes like this:

An "index" is nonarbitrary and unintentional: a print in the mud where a deer has been.

An "icon" is nonarbitrary and intentional: a hoof print drawn on a cave wall, to represent a deer.

A "symbol" is an arbitrary indicator: "deer," and everything else we call a word.

These emerge with the propulsive logic of evolution: a light-sensitive nerve butterflying into an eyeball. A people telling stories in sounds, then glyphs, then letters. And then an endless series of ones and zeros, or however they're doing it these days.

In your little blue bedroom, you'd begun your epic about the fortune teller and the illusionist.

The fortune teller is a fraud who doesn't know it; the illusionist thinks he's a con but is actually the real deal. Together they suffer increasingly elaborate adventures in 1890s New York City.

"Should we be writing this stuff down?" I'd always ask.

Nah, you'd always tell me. *This is just a draft.*

Your characters' shenanigans were mostly comic, though the scene where the illusionist realizes he's actually made his beloved disappear was really quite sad.

Eventually I'd tell you it was late, that I really had to leave. You'd say that I just had to hear what happened next, that the very best part was right around the corner. I'd accuse you of trying to Scheherazade me into staying—to which you'd reply, *I absolutely am*.

Then you'd ask me to stay for just one more chapter—tell me that my presence was really *so* helpful as you organized your thoughts—and anyway, if I didn't read your story, then who would? Though, to your credit, you kept these sorts of maneuvers to a minimum. I'd agree to one more chapter, and then you'd go on to describe the clean blanking smell of the steam, the shallow sleep of an underheated boarding house, the way only certain kinds of fights unsettle horses on the street.

"How do you know these things?" I asked you once.

You looked at me, amazed, and said: *I don't.*

Chapter 10

IN JANUARY IT GOT cold for real, and the mood in your little room grew restless. I'd moved behind you by then—we found everything went faster this way—and our shorthand was growing denser, more specific. "We're an isolate!" I told you once. "Like Basque!"—though any real linguist would have scoffed. I meant it figuratively, I suppose: we were an island language, politically besieged. The S key was becoming a central feature—it never meant "sincere," though it never meant "sarcasm," either; you seemed to use it when you didn't want me to know exactly what you meant. *It stands for subtext,* you said once when I pointed this out. *I thought that was pretty obvious.*

It was becoming clear we needed a project, some new way to focus our energies. The Center had lost some funding around the new year, so the grant subsidizing my work was gone; though I'd agreed to stay on at my previous rate, I told myself it wasn't right to be taking your mother's money at all if I wasn't moving you meaningfully forward. And after the astonishment of your breakthrough, I had to admit that we'd been coasting.

I arrived at our next session full of early-career-professor pep, declaring that it was never too early to start thinking about your future.

Don't you mean it's never too late? you said.

"That, too," I said, then launched into a motivational

monologue about how there was always more to learn. About how you couldn't let your pride—which had served you so well thus far—calcify into arrogance. About how you needed to keep your eye on the big mysteries, and maintain a sense of wonder before them. You went supremely still during all of this, conveying an attitude I could only presume was sardonic. I wasn't used to being behind you yet; I was realizing how much I'd relied on access to your face.

Yikes, you said when I'd finished. *Does that speech work on your students?*

With some dignity, I said that this was *not* a speech I gave to my students (though it was excerpted from a speech I gave myself from time to time). I told you we didn't need to figure everything out just yet. We didn't need to decide right then and there about high school, or the GED, or college. (*Oxford*, you said. *Cambridge. The Sorbonne!*) We only needed to find something interesting, some question you did not know the answer to.

We agreed you'd start with Chekhov.

"Oh hey, it's snowing," I said a few nights later. "I thought maybe it never would again."

I wasn't supposed to be talking to you. I was supposed to be letting you think about Chekhov. Outside, the snowflakes were catching red in the streetlights. The traffic on the way over had been awful, and I was pretty sure I had a low-grade fever. Still, I was aware that this, exactly this, would be the very best part of my day—a fact that had stopped surprising me, though it did occasionally make me feel obscurely sad.

Is it true the Eskimos have a hundred words for snow? you wrote.

An obvious maneuver: you didn't want to be working on that essay either, and you knew I couldn't stand not answering direct questions. I'd once stayed on the phone with a consumer survey for almost an hour, until the telemarketer herself said she really had to go.

"A lot of people think that," I said. "But actually, it's only twenty."

Outside, the snow was turning blue now, falling with the steady certainty of a stage direction. It was beginning to erase your street's dinginess: the buckled sidewalks, the yard with its many scattered paper plates. The bright red Santa hat that had been lodged in a storm drain since before Christmas. All of it muted now, partially paled.

"The categories," I ventured, "pertain to quality of snow, snow formations, transition to water, areas covered with snow . . ."

So what's lacking in volume is made up for in specificity, you said.

"Well, when you really think about it," I said, and stopped.

Yes? you said.

I stared at your neck, where hair wisped into nape; it felt odd that I'd come to know so intimately a part of your body that you couldn't even see.

"Nothing," I said. "I mean, why would you, you know?"

Because it's interesting? you said. *Because I'm dying of suspense?*

You'd turned your head almost toward me; your face wasn't any closer than usual, but it somehow seemed like your mouth was.

"But can a person really care about this question?" I think I was actually asking. "I mean, could there be information any less relevant to the living of a human life?"

I guess it depends on what kind of life you're living, you said, and I turned away from you to laugh. Outside, your street was nearly gone. It was easy to imagine this obscuring as a form of revelation: not the temporary disappearance of the world, but a glimpse of its underlying nature.

Your hand was moving again, I realized.

But I can see why someone would care.

And all of a sudden you were staring straight at me, with an expression of unbearable lucidity on your face. I looked down, then away, then back at you. Your eyes were still right there.

"It turns out to be comparable to the number of English words for 'rain,'" I said abruptly, and stood up. Then I sat back down again, because of course we couldn't talk that way.

Ah.

"We've got around twenty of those," I said. "So, you know, I mean, same deal. Like, 'puddle,' 'drizzle,' 'sleet,' you know. Etcetera."

Etcetera. Sure. And so what do you think that means?

I desperately hoped you were not humoring me.

Are you humoring me? I almost asked.

Never, you almost wrote.

"I think it means we name the things we need to name," I told you. "I think it means we name the things we see."

But then Icelandic has three words for coelacanth, so figure that one out.

At the end of February, you said: *Moira's coming home next month.*

I'd seen this on the calendar. March was an agitated-looking bison, and the second week of the month had "MOIRA!" and a smiley face written on it in bright red letters.

"Oh?" I said. "I guess I'd known that."

I waited for you to go on, but it seemed that you were finished. It had been a strained and silent afternoon; you were, I figured, feeling sour about the essay. "A sophisticated meditation on narrative temporality," I'd called it earlier, while you were working on your outline. You'd told me this was jargon, and I'd said exposure to jargon was necessary practice for academia. That it should be required immunization, like the MMR vaccine! You hadn't spoken to me for a while after that.

"Your sister will be excited by your progress," I said now.

You must know that I despise when you say things like that.

"Like what?" I said. I couldn't tell whether you meant this cutely.

Fake stuff like that, you wrote. So not cute, I gathered.

"Fake stuff," I said. "OK. So she *won't* be excited by your progress, then?"

It's just that that's not how you describe a human emotion.

"Well, we can't all be *writers*."

In the kitchen, your mother put on some bouncy music: one of those baby boomer songs that everyone knows the words to but me. *Human emotion* blinked inauspiciously before us on the screen.

I mean who are you even talking to when you say things like that? you wrote. *You sound like a press release.*

"You," I declared, "are in a weird and wretched mood."

Oh, heavens, weird and wretched??? I was aiming for brooding and unfathomable.

"Well, whatever it is, it's unpleasant."

Which is why you get paid the big bucks, right? To deal with all my . . . unpleasantness?

A thorny subject already, my employment status: the fact that I was paid for every moment I spent with you.

An unpleasantness that today, as you say, takes the form of wretchedness.

"And why is that?" I asked you quietly.

Do I need another reason?

"No," I said. "I'm just wondering if you have one."

Below us, your mother turned up the volume, and, in spite of your pissiness, I could feel you restraining the impulse to bop along a little. It occurred to me that it was very strange to be straddling a person you were fighting with.

So what if I do, you wrote. *I don't have to tell you everything.*

"No."

You don't tell me everything.

"That is true."

You were still once more. It seemed a committed sort of silence. Outside, it was one of those late-February days: flat silver-dollar light, a sense of everything somehow dripping. A feeling not of change, but the prophecy of change. John the Baptist in the desert, or wherever it was he was.

("You know why I take him to concerts?" your mother asked me once.

She was sitting in the kitchen as I packed up my things, a snarl of shadow obscuring her face.

"It's because I want to really know I'm hearing what he's hearing," she said. "That we've got the exact same thing in our ears. And the only thing it's saying is whatever it makes you feel. And there's no way to explain that anyway."

I told her I knew exactly what she meant.

"Yeah?" She looked surprised. "With music?"

With music, sure, I told her. But other things were like that, too.

"Yeah?" she said again. "I guess a few." Her face curled toward a wink. "But I dunno. It's been a while.")

I leaned into you now and said, "I have a daughter."

You stiffened against me and said: *You do?*

"Josephine." Her name came out like an apology. "She's five. She likes Curious George. And candy, and, and, the My Little Ponies. She's afraid of the bath mat, currently." I thought for a moment and added: "She almost never gets cold."

Strong character, you wrote. *I'm cold almost all the time.*

"There's a French word for a person like that," I said. "*Frilleux.*"

I won't try to spell that.

"Also I live with my mother."

Such people inspire my most incandescent contempt.

"Well, you have a good reason."

It sounds like you do too.

"I do. Or, I don't know, I did," I said. You'd dropped your right hand to the side; I lifted it back up for you. It must have bothered your body, the amount of time you spent hunching over the device—I know it gave me all kinds of trouble, and I didn't have to bend as far as you did—but you never, never talked about it.

"Anyway," I said. "It's just a current reality."

A current reality, you said. *See, that one I like. It sounds like something Donald Rumsfeld would say.*

To this, I made no reply.

So, Josephine, you wrote. *OK. I look forward to making her acquaintance.*

"And I look forward to meeting Moira," I said, to make things seem formal and fair. Because this was something that happened when you spent a lot of time with a person: you sometimes met their family.

Sure, you said, and I watched a faint tidal flicker go rolling from the bulb of your head toward your spine. *But I really mean it about Josephine. I really hope someday I'll meet her.*

I took your other hand then, the one we didn't use for typing.

"I would really like that, too," I said.

*

Did I understand what was happening? For a while, I tried to call it something else. Intellectual euphoria, briefly, then—for a long time—friendship. But it was a mistake, it seemed, to call it anything at all, because the wrong names so violently suggested the right one.

Aristotle says the mind understands every entity in terms of four questions: What brought it about? What's it made of? What shape does it have? What's it for? I ran through these, in those early days, trying to ascertain what was actually before me. But this, too, proved unhelpful.

What brought it about? It was there already.

What's it made of? More than its constituent parts.

What shape does it have? Unclear. Vast. Occupying dimensions we don't and probably shouldn't live in.

What's it for? Nothing. No good whatsoever could come of this.

Though it didn't occur to me that nobody would believe me, I knew that nobody would ever, ever understand.

Chapter 11

INDEX TO ICON, ICON to symbol: my interest in this question was becoming largely metaphorical. And yet I thought of it more intensely as weeks burned down to days, and you and I moved ever closer. As our touch became less—more?—than purely utilitarian. As I doubted this at times—for can we always be entirely sure about intention? Language is when someone paints the hoof, and means the deer. But what if the deer just steps in paint, and walks directly onto the wall?

In an epistemologically imperfect world, every belief is a guess. Which makes every action a bet. And one day, in the first week of March, I made one of my own. I let my hand stay on yours, even though I sensed you were done speaking.

And then—already—you were breathing a little faster. I'd become adept at noticing your minute physiological movements—a muscle glimmering taut along your jawline, a subtle pulsar of energy down your arm: these had come to serve as a sort of subtext to our conversations over the months. The change I was registering now was probably extremely small, I told myself; at any rate, I couldn't presume to know what it meant. We'd been talking about Japanese locational terms—maybe that had gotten you going. But then you placed your other hand on mine, and your shoulders fell in a way that seemed decisive—some assertion, some relenting, I didn't know. This was no longer subtext, though neither was it any explicit declaration: this was some other substrate of communication altogether. A tonal indicator in a tonal language: all those nonsemantic signifiers that make certain meanings possible at all.

And then I touched your chest. And then you touched my face. And each step felt like a question, yes—but really, when does it not? And then you kissed me—or somehow, we were kissing. This was a kiss to drown in; a kiss to make you feel all right about just calling it a day and packing up your things. Or anyway, it was for me. How could I ever be sure that it was anything for you?

And yet there you were, still kissing me. And for once I didn't believe a single doubt in my head.

A fade-out here will invite certain accusations; some, I am sure, will see it as yet another reason to doubt me. But those people wouldn't have believed me anyway, because nobody ever believes a sex scene. There is always that feeling of evasion and sanitization, bravado and grandiosity. The crippling awareness of the author's awareness of their own audience. I would never be able to get things exactly right, and this would inevitably inspire dark suspicions about what, exactly, I was getting wrong. And *you* would not believe me, either, because you were actually there: the unavoidable clichés, either clinical or pornographic, would seem insufficient and diminishing. And so any truths I can manage will seem inevitably like deceit; most of the truths I cannot manage at all. I am not, at the end of the day, a writer of stories.

But I suppose that isn't the only problem, if I am being honest. For I have underdescribed your physicality from the start: a radical rarity for a love story. Isn't this what a romance is supposed to be—a breathless catalogue of features and gestures? How his hands were like this and his eyes were like that, and when he took off his glasses you could see that they were even more so? How the first time you touched was when he handed you that pencil or whatever, and in the warmth of his hand you felt the first intuition of what love might be, and how touch could be its conveyance, etc., etc.? Or maybe all of that came later, when he grabbed and kissed you in a rainstorm, smelling like X and tasting like Y and all of this provoking physiological response Z, and you felt around you the kind of rollicking, Biblical frenzy that seems to tell you something definitive about the universe?

I, personally, am bored already.

There is the arrogance of describing you, yes; there's also the vapidity. Why recount trivialities, when every essential thing about you is obscured by such descriptions? And partly—mostly?—my hesitation is more selfish. Because the sooner you become a sequence of gestures, the sooner you are reduced to them in my memory: made into a series of pat little predicates, unfurling in some disembodied loop in my mind.

But it isn't that I cannot do it. I could tell of the way your hand tended to churn in a sort of etcetera type of motion—which sometimes felt like you were encouraging me to go on, and other times reminding me that you'd heard it all already—or the way you'd sometimes curl that same hand in front of you, primly, in an odd little feline gesture. There was that frantic, frenetic energy between us whenever we got too close: the kind of electricity that both people might try to privately mischaracterize, but that neither could deny existed. There was the matter of your long, sharp-angled body; your pale, notably ovular face; your eyes, nameless-dark and depthless and yet somehow always winking. You had long, bony, extremely graceful fingers (*Never worked a day in my life*, you liked to say). You made a sort of throttled chirping noise when excited, often during sex, and I'll admit this startled me a bit at first. Isn't this the kind of disclosure that the people are all waiting for? My observations about your body and condition—my fucking *field notes?* Well, as far as I'm concerned, they can have them. This stuff isn't a secret: it just doesn't matter enough to be.

Did we not live in a world, and you in a body? We did, you did. I adored them both for containing you. In your absence, neither is particularly dear to me. Another way of putting this is that I loved you for your mind—a dopey tautology that only people with minds not worth loving could ever understand as an insult.

Later, after you were sleeping, I stared at your popcorn ceiling. I was remembering my own childhood bedroom's confounding wallpaper: skeins of blue half-clovers against a white backdrop, worryingly distorted at the seams. I remembered, in one particularly morbid season of my childhood, trying to use those flowers to gauge the length of my probable remaining lifespan. Would I live as many hours as there were flowers on this wall? I asked my mother. Would I? Would she? Would I? This must have been around the time my father died.

Yes, she told me, though it's possible she hadn't calculated things very carefully.

"And what if they were days?" I said. "Or months? Or years?"

She looked around the room and said, "Well, maybe not quite that many."

My love for you moved something like that: shifting its units in exponential, terrifying leaps. Does that make any sense? It doesn't, really. It didn't to me, even then.

But maybe that's what all love is like—indescribable, utterly resistant to metaphor. Maybe this is the entire point.

And so love had come to me, and the context was not perfect. There was ridicule ahead of us, and vast incomprehension; there were inconveniences coming, and sacrifice, and doubt.

But give anyone in the world this prophecy, they'll only hear the first few words: *love has come to me, love has come to me, love has come to me, at last.*

Part II

Chapter 12

IT's SUMMER NOW, AT last, improbably. Fretful nights too hot to sleep, half dreams turning above me like a baby's mobile. The feeling reminiscent of certain febrile childhood deliriums. We didn't have an air conditioner then, either.

"This is crazy," I told you the second time it happened.

It is, you said.

The third time, I said: "I didn't mean for things to be this way."

I did, you said. *I've been meaning it since you walked through the door.*

The fourth time, I said, "I'm sorry I couldn't be more professional."

You said, *Please don't start patronizing me now.*

The fifth time, I said, "But this is so insane!"

We were half-clothed and breathless, our bodies still touching at weird junctures: my hip against your thigh, your arm around my waist; my foot, for some reason, largely underneath your ass. The device sat between us, as frank and ludicrous as sex itself.

You're going to hurt my feelings if you keep saying that, you wrote.

"No," I said. I lifted your fingers to kiss them each. "When I say it's crazy, I mean." And then: "You *know* what I mean."

You gave me a look like: *Do I?*—and shoved up and away from me a little. This kind of maneuver took a lot out of you, so you must have really meant it. My feet and hands were cold now; I pressed my hip into your thigh. The device rested mutely between us.

"Please say something," I said, and sat up. I placed the device in front of you, then curled around behind you so I could hold your hands again.

I mean, you said finally. *Is it really that incredible?* You were hitting the keys, I thought, a little harder than usual; once or twice I found myself nearly ejected. *Is it really so confoundingly jaw-dropping that someone could ever love me?*

"No." I stilled your hands to stop you from going on. "My God, no. Of course not."

I bent down and kissed your wrist, then I leaned around and kissed your mouth. Here was the room I wanted to die in. I wished only to close the door behind me.

"Anyway," I said, after some time. "I didn't say I *loved* you."

I know, you said. *You didn't have to.*

Omenie: Romanian for the virtue of being fully human.

We don't have this one in English.

"JoJo's pulling out her hair again," my mother said a few nights later.

"*Again?*" I said.

We were standing over the sink, scooping great mounds

of falafel onto plates. It was one of those warmish late winter evenings when the temperature careens toward fifty; you see people walking around with hats in hands, with hands out of pockets. Until mere moments ago, I believe I had been humming.

"Yes," my mother said, hoisting the final mound with her spatula. "There was that whole episode last winter?"

I tried to recall last winter. I had just started at the lab. Peter had been gone six months—less—and my period wasn't even back yet. I'll admit this time is a bit of a blur.

"Maybe she needs therapy," I said.

"Don't be funny," my mother said.

It was a running joke in our family how we could never quite afford the services we were marginally paid to provide for others.

"Well, maybe I should get her a surprise or something," I said. From the living room, I could hear JoJo and Alan playing that dumb hand-slapping game where the kid always loses. The game is rigged, kid! I wanted to shout at her. I don't know why she put up with it. "She liked that dolphin thing so much."

"Hm," my mother said, and wiped a soppy hair across her forehead. It was, for some reason, approximately one thousand degrees in our house.

"Wait a minute," I said. "Where *is* that dolphin?"

My mother grabbed the plastic pitcher from the cupboard and began filling it with water. "I threw it out," she said.

"What?"

"She peed right on it."

"*What?* Why?"

"Why? Because she wet the bed, and that damn dolphin was in it."

She poured a packet of pink Crystal Light into the pitcher and began stirring with the clean end of the spatula.

"Oh," I said. In the other room, Jo cackled at some remark of Alan's. A pun, no doubt: the lowest form of humor. "Well, couldn't you have cleaned it?"

"I'm sure someone could have," my mother said, and sailed airily out of the kitchen.

Later, over dinner, my mother inquired brightly if I'd given any thought to going back to school.

"Some thought, sure," I said, and swallowed. It was a common tactic of my mother's to interrogate me in front of witnesses, hemming me into my more socially acceptable evasions.

"It's getting to be that time of year," she added.

"March already!" Alan said, and whistled. "It sure doesn't feel like it."

"Every year we delude ourselves into the fantasy that March is spring," I said severely. "Every year, it is not."

Though today had actually been quite mild. After work, I'd walked a half a mile I didn't need to, dawdling like a child over my mother's request for milk.

"But Easter," said Josephine.

"That's in April this year," I said.

We all fell silent, considering this fact. The falafel was very dry, and Alan—not known for masticating swiftly under the best of circumstances—chewed for an extremely long time.

"Did you ever write back to that man who sent you the book?" my mother asked.

For a moment my tongue stuck to the roof of my mouth. I flashed to a memory of the messiest kid in second grade, tongue affixed to frozen pole, howling as the teacher poured warm water to release her. She was the class wretch, attention starved in a way I now recognize as suggesting a truly dark backstory, and too disastrously dumb (I believed at the time) to think it through when the other kids had dared her. But later I wondered if maybe she had, and did it anyway, just for the moment when everyone had to watch her march up to that pole. She must have felt terrifying then, commanding real suspense among her enemies: What is this person capable of, and what have I provoked her to do, and what will befall us all if she actually does it? Maybe this made the whole thing worth it, regardless of the aftermath.

"What?" I said, unsticking. "Oh, you mean *Tyruil?* God no."

"It was nice of him to think of you," my mother said.

"I assure you, it was not."

"It seemed like it might have been a sort of overture."

"It was purely a taunt."

My mother stood abruptly then to clear her dish—Alan's, too, although he was definitely still eating—and fled the room.

Alan looked at me. A small bolus bulged in his cheek—falafel, presumably—and I had the sense he wasn't quite sure what to do with it.

"She's just worried about you," he said, with some difficulty. Behind him, the kitchen door was still swinging.

"But why?" I said. "I'm fine. I have a job. I find my work rewarding. JoJo, eat your peas. The Easter Bunny is keeping very careful track."

Or was it only Santa who was meant to have such all-seeing powers? JoJo, hedging her bets, shoveled an enormous spoonful of peas into her mouth. A Pascal's wager: smart kid. I ruffled her hair a bit.

"I was very grateful to you, Alan, for helping me get started."

"Well." The bolus, though diminished, had not entirely disappeared. "I was pleased to be of assistance."

I laughed and said, "You sound *extremely* pleased," and that's when Alan finally, finally swallowed.

"I was sorry to see about Leana, that's all."

He wiped his napkin, several times, along his upper lip.

"Leana?" I had no idea what he was talking about, although my first impulse was to pretend I did. Deception becoming a reflex, already. Instead I said, "I hadn't heard anything about Leana."

Alan sat back in his chair and said, "Oh." There was still half a chickpea on his lip, but it seemed cruel to mention this in light of his recent exertions.

"Alan, what happened?"

"Oh, it's. Well, you know."

"I don't, in fact."

"There've been some—issues with her research, apparently."

"Oh?"

"She had to retract an article."

"She did?"

"You really didn't hear?" said Alan. He looked wretched and neurasthenic, though that was absolutely typical. "There was a whole thing about it in the *Globe*. It made that whole kind of therapy look—well, it all looked pretty bad."

"Not her article about Nelly?" I said. "Nelly could recite Dickinson." It was "I'm Nobody, Who Are You?" Which was maybe a tasteless choice, in retrospect. I knew Leana had been submitting that paper to the real journals, though I hadn't known it had been published.

"I really don't know, Angela."

"Why are you *whispering?*"

"I'm not sure your mother wanted me to say anything."

"You just said it was in the *Globe*!" I said, and Alan winced. "You know, Alan, I appreciate everything you've done for us. I really do. But I have to say, I'm getting pretty sick of all the Court of Versailles stuff around here."

From the kitchen came the sounds of my mother's angriest dishwashing, eruptions of rage clattering followed by long soggy silences. Alan thumbed contemplatively at the tablecloth.

"Then I will be direct with you," he said after a moment. "I find it hard to see a future for you in this line of work."

"Ah," I said, and stabbed a renegade chickpea with my fork. "Well, the great thing, Alan, is that you don't have to. In fact, you don't have to personally visualize anything for me at all. I think if you and my mother can try to keep that in mind, you'll both cheer up considerably."

"And when Easter comes," said Josephine, and Alan and I looked at her. I think we'd both sort of forgotten she was there.

"That, too, will be cheering," I said.

"*If* you finish your peas," my daughter amended sternly, and I wondered if this is what I sounded like to her. How did the child not laugh me to scorn every single day of my life?

"Well, I'm not sure poor Alan really had a chance," I said, looking poor Alan straight in his eyeballs. "I bet your plate's still in the kitchen, though. She never throws out food."

"I *know* that," said Alan, standing and giving me a strange long look. Then he went obediently into the kitchen to file his report.

One thing all truths have in common: they are only visible from certain distances.

I found myself reflecting on this later that evening, after all the other people in my house had gone to sleep. Alone in my room, I turned Tyruil's smug little book around; its anonymous, unbecoming backside was facing out now. *An overture*, I thought, and shuddered. Now it was just papers in a binding, just words upon a page. Then I reopened Nabokov, for consolation and for spite.

Pale Fire—anyone will tell you—has the feel of an optical illusion. This sense is partly thematic—the ongoing motif of glass and mirrors, doppelgangers and reflections: the communion of the viewer with the viewed. But partly the effect is conjured by the very act of reading. We can stand back and grasp the general architecture—here is a self-serving narrator, hijacking the footnotes of an epic poem in or- der to tell the tale of the deposed king of Zembla—or we can dizzy ourselves by leaning into the fretwork: delight- ing over details, the sly recurrences and almost anagrams. But in the end, *Pale Fire* is most elusive when viewed from some middle distance: you can see the face or you can see the vase, but you can never see them both at once. And this is where most people would just give up.

It will not spoil *Pale Fire* to say it hinges on the ques- tion of whether its narrator, Charles Kinbote, is in fact the king of Zembla. He certainly seems to want us to think so, although he never says so, even as the textual evidence mounts around him. (So maybe it's Nabokov who wants us to think so, one could be forgiven for thinking, before one had thought about it a little more.) But then, there in the footnotes, up pops one V. Botkin, a minor colleague of the epic poet John Shade, and an almost anagram of Kinbote; perhaps the narrator was only a delusional academic all along, we think, a truth hidden in plain sight for any reader willing to squint hard enough. But squint a little harder, and the vision changes yet again. We know from the text that the Zemblan language draws heavily from German and Russian; *kin*, the novel tells us, is the Zemblan word for "king"; *bot*, if written in capital letters and read in Cyrillic, is Russian for "here." A plausible translation of Botkin, then: "Here is king." The articles dropped, as they would be in a Slavic language.

And could this really be a coincidence—from Nabokov, trickster god of multilingual wordplay? Yet there's no reason to think this answer is definitive—that there aren't ever-smaller portals to discover behind many other obscured doors—or that Nabokov cared if we ever found them. Of course he didn't care. What other people understood was not among his interests.

I, however, was not most other people. I was capable of sustaining vast complexities—more than the usual person, certainly, and absolutely more than your average reader of the *Boston Globe*. I wasn't going to read the article, I decided. Or if I did, I wasn't going to care about what it said. I could believe, of course, that Leana had made some mistakes. It's just that this had nothing whatsoever to do with you and me.

I might have even explained some of this to Alan, if I'd thought there was any chance at all he'd understand.

Chapter 13

It wasn't that I had no ethical objections whatsoever. But then, they really only went so far.

It was a lot like a professor dating a student, I decided— this was truly the best analogy. There are reasons, very good ones, why such a relationship is considered inadvisable. There's a structural imbalance that can lead to misbehavior, coercion, poor judgment. There's a distortion in professionalism—for this is *very* unprofessional—that is likely to make other people uncomfortable. There's the likelihood of diminished credibility for all involved. The taboo against teacher-student entanglement stems from the norm that, on average, such a relationship is less likely to be equal. It is less likely to be fair. It is less likely, at the end of the day, to be love. This is a conclusion derived from a welter of conventional morality and liability projections and cost-benefit analyses, an anonymous collective saying, "We don't know you, but if we had to guess, we'd disapprove."

And yet everyone will admit there are exceptions. The guidelines are not equipped to know which ones they are.

It seemed fair that I might leave my job—not as penance, but as the price of a certain sort of freedom. Beyond that, we were only humans: unconventional, yes, statistically inadvisable, absolutely—but also certain of our love, certain that we were doing no harm.

*

The second week of March, Moira returned from Chicago.

She showed up on the porch right after lunch. She was slight, with sandy-colored hair, wearing jeans and stripy sneakers and those overstated hipster glasses one was starting to see everywhere those days. She was lugging an enormous suitcase—I wondered how long she planned to stay—and it thunked up the stairs behind her, sending shards of ice skittering.

"Let me help you with that," I said, once she was already mostly inside.

"I got it." She stood and adjusted her glasses. "You must be the miracle worker."

"Angela," I said, extending my hand.

"Right." She leaned toward me to shake it. She had brought the smell of the cold inside with her. Somehow, we were exactly the same height. "Moira."

"Right!" I said, stepping back a little. "It must be your spring break!"

Though of course I knew that already. My gaze spun around the kitchen. I wanted to offer her something—but this seemed odd, in her own childhood home.

"Well, it's great to finally meet you!" I chirped instead. "I've heard so much about you."

"Oh yeah?" said Moira. "From whom?"

At this, I winced a little. Not being a prescriptivist, myself.

"From your mother," I told her. "And Sam, of course."

"From Sam, huh?" She traced a seam in the linoleum with her sneaker. "And just what exactly did he have to say?"

"Just, you know. How great you are," I said. "How much he's looking forward to seeing you. And to talking with you, obviously!"

I was aware this sounded fake—as though this generic praise was covering for some specific nastiness. In fact, you hadn't said that much about Moira at all, and I was wishing I hadn't ventured any of this.

"Yes," said Moira, adjusting her glasses once again. Up close, I could see that the frames were flecked with pink. Her eyes, though dark like yours, were significantly less winking. "I am looking forward to that as well."

"Can I get you anything?" I asked. "Water, or, I think there's seltzer in the fridge."

"I remember where it is," she said, but made no move toward moving. I felt I understood the frustration an animal experiences when some higher species finds its submission rituals illegible.

"Your bag seems pretty heavy," I observed.

"It's mostly books," she said. "Some new CDs for Sammy."

"You have to take that many books home with you on break?"

I had no idea why I was assuming the posture of some dumbfounded village matriarch. I had been in attendance at a rigorous academic institution myself, only very recently.

"I brought a lot of them for *fun*," your sister told me kindly. "I like to read."

"Oh yes!" I cried. "I do too."

"Oh yeah?" Your sister brushed her bangs across her

forehead. She had a faint arrow-shaped scar above her left eyebrow—it was from biking into a mailbox, you told me later. "And what have you been reading lately?"

"I've been revisiting Nabokov," I said. "Most recently."

I was aware of speaking with a certain wounded stateliness.

"Nice. *Lolita?*"

"*Pale Fire.*"

"*Very* cool," your sister said, and from her tone I could tell she had not read it.

Then the cuckoo clock struck two, and I jumped about a mile.

"That thing," said Moira, to keep the peace. And then we laughed together, for exactly as long as we had to.

Over the months, your mother had grown comfortable with my role as translator. I think in some ways she preferred it. Partly this was due to her skittishness with the device, which she continued to regard as one of those unfathomable technologies best left to the very young. Though your mother always talked about your condition as though she understood it, it's true she didn't always act that way. She still hung back babyishly at the beginning of our conversations, like a child visiting a diseased grandparent in the hospital. "Please stay," she'd whispered to me once, when I'd tried to give you two some privacy—even though you were sitting right there and could hear her as well as I could.

It's true I sometimes wondered if your mother was being a bit evasive—if she wasn't in any hurry to speak to you individually, with whatever revelations and recriminations that might entail. But that was OK too, I figured—you two were still getting to know each other, and there would be plenty of time to say whatever needed to be said. In any case, your mother hadn't asked again to speak to you directly—though she often spoke about speaking to you, in some friendly short-term nonspecific future.

But Moira's arrival had changed all that. In the weeks before her return, your mother had launched plans for a great unveiling. And this made sense, when you thought about it. Your doctors all said the same thing: the technology was too experimental; they were unable to assess any improvements that relied on it (though one of them added, simperingly, that he was in favor of any rituals that might improve caretaker morale). Who, then, besides Moira, could recognize how far you'd come? I sometimes wondered if there was a bit of defensiveness afoot, too. Moira—regional defector, first-generation college attendee, off studying incomprehensible subjects, then flying to Guatemala for Christmas, thank you very much!— well, she wasn't the only one in this family who'd been up to something. She wasn't the only one whose life had changed! Though it's possible that here I am just projecting.

Either way, with Moira's arrival came renewed interest in what your mother called "A Serious Conversation"—a phrase she deployed with ominous frequency as the date of your sister's return drew near. *You* kept calling the whole thing a test: a test you should not have to pass in order to have your family believe that you existed.

"So don't think of it as a test," I told you one afternoon.

You'd been tasked, as usual, with Chekhov. I'd been half expecting you to launch into your fortune teller saga instead—inspiration tending to strike most insistently when other work was at hand. *Ah! The inconstant nature of the Muse!* you liked to say—and I'd say she actually seemed to be extremely constant, if a person was paying any attention.

But it is a test, you said now, quite reasonably. We were sitting on your bed, the device upon my lap. Outside, there was that icy first-spring light through the window, the dawning canticle of early rush-hour traffic.

"OK," I said. "But that's not the only thing a person might call it."

It's a test! you said. *It's a pop quiz and an ambush.*

"Think of it as . . . an introduction," I said. "Or, I don't know. A performance!"

I made that little half bow with a cascading hand flourish people do when they're trying to seem courtly. You regarded this coldly out of the corner of your eye.

I am not in possession of the performative instinct, you wrote.

"*No* performative instinct? Really?" I was irritated now. Because making a fool of oneself is always a gesture of goodwill; to use it as any sort of opening is simply petty. "You wrote an entire book about a stage magician. You typed it out while I watched!"

That is fiction, Angela, you wrote. *That is not about me.*

"Well, can you think of this as fiction, then? Some kind of story that you're telling?"

Can I do that, Angela? Can I summon the capacity to narratively dissociate in this manner?

You never usually used rhetorical questions. I think you found them tacky.

I just don't know, Angela! You never normally used my name either, I was realizing. I wondered what that meant. *I have simply never tried!*

"I do grasp what you're saying," I said. "But definitely don't let that stop you, if you're having fun."

I lowered my head a little, in preparation for a whole lot more of this, but instead you fell still and stayed that way.

"What, that's it?" I said after a moment, lifting my head up to your ear. "Maybe you really *don't* have a performative instinct."

You shook your head a little. In what attitude, I couldn't say. Your hair was getting long—incipiently curly, the way I loved it—which meant your mother would probably cut it within the week. On an impulse, I kissed a curl. Your shoulders slumped.

I think the worst part is, she obviously doesn't even really want to do it. Your mother, I assumed. *It's just she's terrified of Moira.*

"You don't need to worry about Moira," I said. "You leave Moira up to me."

I didn't say I was worried, you said. *I never worry.*

A common boast of yours, though I never did believe it.

I just don't want to sit there and be a prop in some scene.

I squeezed your hand and said, "I promise there will be no scenes."

No scenes? Your shoulders clenched a little, a gesture I'd come to understand as your darkest demonstration of amusement. *Do you remember December? Every time she touched me, you could hear the fucking strings!*

It was true. You were right. If I listened closely, I could hear them even now.

"This time will be different," I said. "Your mother was— overwhelmed back then. She's more used to things these days."

To this, you did not respond. I gathered myself up and waited. I'd often wondered why you never really gave me the silent treatment in our fighting. It would have been so easy.

I just didn't think I'd have to do this stuff anymore, you said at last. *I thought that was the point of all of this.*

The point of all what, I wanted to say. The point of what? Another part of me wanted to say that change never comes so cleanly. Tendrils, inflections of the past will stay with you a while—might stay with you forever!—like an accent that never disappears, only fades until no one can tell where you're from. The biggest part of me just wanted to kiss you, but a smaller, louder part was aware how this could seem: like a manipulation, or a threat, or a bribe. I wanted to believe we were past that sort of thinking, but I also knew that trust between two humans was extremely fragile—now was not the time to make assumptions.

And so the part of me that was actually operative said: "I don't know how to get you out of it. I've thought about it for a while, and I'm sorry, I just don't."

I stood and took a little lap around your room. Outside, the snow was beginning to melt, receding into

ill-defined dirt-striped clumps, ringed at the edges by
ice. The paper plates were reappearing, and that maud-
lin Virgin Mary, and all the other things that had been
there all along.

I sat back down and said, "We need to be talking about
the future."

Oh, this, already, you wrote. *Sorry, babe. You're great and
all, but.*

"And it might as well be now," I said. "While you're mad
at me already."

*I'm a rolling stone! Playas gonna play, etc. Am I doing this
part right?*

"I'm thinking we should talk about—about the GED,
obviously. And college, of course."

Yeah? You gonna move into the dorm with me or what?

"There are lots of ways that we can—"

*Because I'm gonna want to join an improv troupe. A cappella,
most definitely. You sure you're up for all of that?*

"I do realize you're joking."

Well, hey! you said. *You really do almost have a PhD.*

I pulled my hand away from yours, then realized this
was not an option. I put it back.

"Is that—is that you trying to hurt my feelings?"

No.

"Because what *would* hurt my feelings is if you were actually that bad at it."

To keep myself from speaking further, I focused on placing teeth on teeth. Your hand was warm beneath my own,

your precious pulse was racing. But all that said was that you felt something; it could never, never tell me what.

"This college thing is not—this is not some kind of—charitable pestering on my part," I said. "I don't think you understand that this is selfish."

I thought all charity was selfish, you wrote. *I thought you philosophy people settled that one.*

"Please don't make me talk abstractly," I said. "I didn't think *I'd* have to do *that* anymore."

You were still again, your pulse frantic with rage or lust or some other emotion I had no name for, and thus (some might argue) could not conceive of. At the very least, it seemed I had your attention.

"I don't want you to have to rely on me," I said. "I want you to have a whole future, a whole world. And partly that's because I, well. Partly it's because I just want those things for you and you should have them. But partly it's because I want you to decide. To be *able* to decide." I was crying now, I realized. "I need to know—I need *them* to know—you're not a hostage."

The crying was for real, and yet some small part of me stood beyond it, aware I'd made a certain move, played a certain card, and curious to see what kind of reaction this would provoke.

"If I can't ever really know that, then I just, I mean, I just." I hiccupped pitifully. The last time I remembered really crying was at Peter's funeral—when crying was not merely permitted, but required. In secret defiance, I'd cried for many things at once. "Then I just can't see *how*, you know?"

You put your arm around me—hoisting it, the way you had to for this sort of gesture. "You put your arm around me": how fond, how innocent, how *chaste* that sounds. When in reality we were at that point where the smell of the other person's *detergent* becomes a provocation. Yours was Tide, and I was pretty allergic to it, actually.

All right, all right, you wrote. *No scenes.*

I wasn't sure if you were asking for a promise for the future, or a mischaracterization of the present.

"All right?" I said. "Really?"—and then you kissed me. Maybe, I realized much later, so you wouldn't have to lie to me again.

Saudade (Portuguese): a feeling of melancholic longing for an irretrievable person or place. Has analogues in Welsh (*hiraeth*) and German (*Sehnsucht*) and perhaps in some combination of our "nostalgia" and "utopia," derived from Greek, especially if we consider that *utopos* originally just meant "nowhere."

Afterward, I said: "You may not be a performer, but you *are* a kind of magician."

I was in that loopy zone where such utterances may occur.

That character isn't a metaphor, you said, and kissed my eyelashes.

"Are you so sure about that?"

No.

"The author's dead!" I cried. "It's official, folks. He's admitted it himself!"

I was punchy, oblivious with relief. I believed we'd either come to some agreement, or else weathered the fact that we could not.

But I can tell you that I am not a metaphor, you said. *And are you so sure you know that?*

I went completely still. In truth, I was never entirely sure about anything—this humility being my one certainty, and perhaps my only grace. Yet even the radical skeptic goes home to his long-suffering family—deigning, for one more evening, to pretend to know that they are real.

"Yes," I said. And then, more loudly, "Yes. I am. I have never believed in anything more fully in my entire life than I do in you. In this."

And this, at least, was true.

Me neither, you said after a while, and I decided to decide to believe this, too.

Chapter 14

A word about my husband.

I did not want to bring him into this. He is dead, and blameless in the matter under discussion; I am glad he's not around to see what's become of me. He would, I think, be very surprised. He'd been astonished by my graduate degree, astonished by my pregnancy (by the female reproductive apparatus generally, with all its Rube Goldberg fussiness). We were extremely young when we got married. We knew quickly, quietly, that we should not have. Perhaps we would have divorced, eventually. But it never came to that.

I was sad for him for dying so young. Later I was sad that he'd never had a chance to love someone the way a person should—if only once, for a very little while, under threat of incarceration. It occurs to me now that I am the only person who knows how lonely he must have been. And now I am left alone with this awful fact, which feels like a secret we were never quite close enough to share.

In all the many ways to tell my story, there is only one I will not countenance. This is the story of a widow so grief-stricken she loses her mind. Say my mind was already lost, say I never had one to begin with. Say my mind is not the problem, but my conscience, my moral compass, my soul. Say any of the hundred things one could say about me, and that many people, I am told, regularly do. It is true that a few people forgive me; somewhat fewer, I have heard, even believe me. But this, I do not expect. All I ask is that we leave poor Peter out of it. It is not his fault for dying—or if it is, it's nobody else's business. And if he'd lived, it would have happened anyway.

The Serious Conversation was attempted the last Friday of spring break.

Your mother had dressed for the occasion; she was wearing a purple paisley blouse and those earrings you'd given her at Christmas. They turned out not to suit her: they were that light green color that makes pale skin look vaguely diphtheric. Your sister stood in the corner, drinking an enormous Slurpee, giving off the unmistakable vibe of a movie critic who absolutely cannot wait to be gravely disappointed.

"Still got your White Sox pennant, buddy?" she said, her tone aggressively rhetorical. This wasn't even a question, really, since she was staring right at it. I'd been afraid Moira would ask to talk to you; I didn't know how juggling two new conversation partners would go, and your sister radiated the kind of academic prickliness I had a hard time saying no to. But Moira had announced, through sips of Slurpee, that she'd rather just watch this time—putting a little spin on "this time" that might have been a joke or might have been a threat or might have been the verbal equivalent of our S key. Or might have actually been nothing, come to think of it.

Your mother arranged herself behind you. "Don't be nervous!" I said, as I reminded her how to position her hands, how to stabilize your elbow.

"I *am* nervous!" said your mother, and laughed with real merriment. I was nervous, too, in fact. There was the problem of your grudging attitude, obviously, as well as my own unseemly investment. There was your mother's breathless posture, as though she was the host of a dinner party during which important matters of state would be discussed. There was your sister and that damn Slurpee, which she snorkeled ever louder, though she never seemed to get any closer to reaching the bottom.

"Can you put that thing in the fridge, Mo?" said your mother.

"Why?" said Moira.

"It's not a problem," I told your sister cheerfully. And then: "Do they not have 7-Elevens in Chicago?"

"They have 7-Elevens *everywhere.*"

She looked at me as though it was my cognition we should be testing.

"Let's get started," I said, in my best Harvard TA voice.

Your mother was straddling you slightly, cradling your elbow in one hand. The pose reminded me of how I used to sit with JoJo in the bathtub, back before she swore off baths—the suction cup objections proving more durable than anticipated.

"Hi, Sam," she said. "It's your mother."

He knows that, I wanted to say but did not.

"I'm going to ask you some questions today, OK, buddy?" She was leaning further into you, and I could sense her taking in your scent. Such a strange impulse, the need to take stock of your child in this way. JoJo smelled like Cheerios and muddy lavender and All Free Clear detergent, the kind they say has no smell but does. "What I mean is, you and I are going to try to have a chat."

She seemed to be waiting for a verbal response from you, or else some kind of physical indication of assent. To give her time to catch herself, I began counting to five in my head.

"Sam knows all that," I said, on the count of four. "He's fine with it."

Though "fine" was obviously not the right word. "Stoically resigned" might have come closer. I'd never spoken about you in front of you—at least, not since the very beginning. I hated that you had to hear me explain you in shorthand.

"Sam," your mother said. Her normal voice was gone already: she was talking straight out of a séance. "How are you feeling today? Are you glad to have Moira back from school?"

She was clutching you oddly, though whether too tremulously or too intensely, I wasn't sure. One of you seemed to be shaking, and I was pretty sure it was her.

At length, your hand moved a bit.

T, you wrote, and your mother looked up at me for translation.

"He probably meant Y," I said. "For 'yes.' Which is the next key over." Although I wasn't sure about this. If you couldn't talk the way you wanted to, I had some doubt you'd even try. "Maybe avoid yes-or-no questions for now?"

Your forefinger was flickering tentatively, in a shivery Morse code not at all like your usual style.

"Shh," said your mother. "He's saying something else

now." Though we didn't need to be quiet to see what you were writing, and nobody was talking anyway. You were squinting at the device in a gaze just short of a glare. Your mother took in a sharp breath and closed her eyes. I wondered with some alarm if she was *praying*.

Ik, you wrote, at long last.

"Ik?" said Moira. "What is 'ik'?"

"'OK,' probably," I said, frowning into the keyboard. "Since the I is right next to the O."

"OK?" said your mother.

"Well, you asked him a second ago how he was doing," I said. "So he was probably responding to that. Can you maybe hold his arm a little tighter?"

"Like this?" your mother said, holding your arm—if it was possible—even more limply than before. She was a tough person in a lot of ways, your mother. I had a great regard for her—really, I still do. Yet she *shrunk* around you in a way I couldn't bear. Someone throwing up her hands before a thing she'd deemed impossible—yet wanting to be seen *trying* to do this impossible thing: oh, just a little, just a little. A damsel tied to the tracks, struggling prettily against her bindings!

"I know we haven't tried this in a while," your mother added meekly.

"It's OK," I said. My voice came out hoarse and somewhat louder than intended; the echo chambers of my face were all messed up somehow. Those sinuses again, I figured. "I know Sam has been extremely grateful for all of your support."

I tried to catch your eye then, to engage you in some private, sardonic glance. These Thanksgiving relatives, can you even *believe* them? But soon they will be gone, and we will do the dishes, and go to bed to talk about them until we fall asleep. That's what's coming, that's what's real—this look is just a promise, a reminder. But somehow I could not seem to get your attention.

"Remember my questions, Mom?" said Moira, suckling at what had to be the last of her Slurpee. "Can you ask him some of those?"

"Oh yes," said your mother vacantly. "Remember our little dog, Sam? He loved you so much." She sounded on the verge of tears. About the dog? I couldn't imagine. "Or—what's your grandmother's middle name? Do you remember the last thing she gave me?"

"I don't know if it's helpful for him to feel like you're quizzing him," I said.

"Isn't that what you do?" said Moira.

"Not exactly," I said.

"What about that song from the diaper commercial?" your mother said. "When you're old enough to go out to the park..."

She began to bop and sway a little.

"Is that—are you trying to make him *dance?*" said Moira. Her tongue by now was extremely purple; it looked like something medical.

"He used to do it all the time," your mother said.

I tapped your mother on the shoulder in a way I hoped was both resolute and gentle. "I think maybe if you try to ask him something open-ended?"

"OK," she said, without turning around, and I could hear that her obedience had already outlasted her faith. In a lot of families, one learns to march right out the door the first time one feels some skepticism of authority—I'd been at Harvard long enough to know. But I wasn't raised in that kind of family, and neither was your mother. And neither, it occurs to me now, were you.

"How is," your mother said, then paused a good long while. "School."

"Want to tell them about your essay, Sam?" I said.

"He's writing an essay?" said your mother, turning.

I cocked my head; I was feeling subaquatic.

"About Chekhov," I said, and your sister snorted.

"Sorry," she said. "Brain freeze."

"Can you tell us about your essay, buddy?" said your mother. Her eyes all of a sudden looked very awake.

"Well, he hasn't finished yet," I said, and your sister made another kind of honking sound: something darker and more clotted.

Se, you were writing. *Ty*.

"Time!" I said. "Exactly. And the sea. That's where this time shift takes place."

You looked flushed, maybe a little alarmed. You still would not meet my gaze. The essay was a sensitive topic under the best of circumstances; perhaps it had been a mistake to bring it up right now.

"I think Sam is getting tired," I said, and this time Moira didn't even bother to snort. She was staring at your keyboard with a look of prudish horror.

"No," your mother said firmly, and Moira and I both looked at her. She was staring intently at the back of your neck, where the fact of your body met the mystery of your mind. She'd made all of it, after all. For you, she'd wait forever.

"No," she said again, more quietly. "Let's keep trying."

English is oddly vigilant about the hypothetical. Languages vary in their explicitness; on this matter, ours is extremely frank.

If you meet Sam, you will understand.

If you met Sam, you would understand.

If you'd have met Sam, you would have understood.

In these phrases, we descend through multiple levels of unreality. The first implies something that hasn't happened yet but still might; the second shifts the situation into the realm of the imagined. The third nudges the entire scenario, complete with its own hypotheticality, into the past: something that might have happened once but did not—and now, we are invited to believe, never will.

Afterward, your mother said: "Drink with me."

We were sitting on the porch. Your mother had brought out a bottle of wine and three glasses—optimistically, I guess, imagining Moira might join us. In the yard across the street, the paper plates glinted: frayed little disks oddly luminous in the moonlight.

"I don't really drink," I said. In fact, I never do. I am extremely vain about my own perceptions. But this is not the sort of thing you should say to people at a party—or in any context, most likely.

"I know you smoke," your mother said.

I laughed and said, "I'm quitting."

"Oh yeah," she said. "Me too. All the time."

She tapped out two Marlboros from her pack. I wasn't picky about brand, myself, though I had a soft spot for the Pall Malls my father began smoking in the Korean War. I didn't remember him, not really, but their smell made me absolutely certain he'd once been around.

Your mother handed me a cigarette, and I leaned in toward her for a light. She always smelled of Pert Plus and chlorine—something like a YMCA women's locker room—though I don't know where the chlorine part came from. She couldn't possibly have had any time to swim.

After a time, your mother said, "You make it look so easy."

I took a drag and said, "It's deceptive that way."

There was a minor leavening in my chest already, and I tried to blow it away into the sky. I could feel you off in your room behind us, despising everyone.

"Huh," your mother said. "So it isn't easy?"

"It's just a really finicky technology," I said. I was aware of speaking just a bit too quickly. "It's a lot about nonverbal cues. Body language. Intuition."

"Intuition, huh."

I took another drag. I was beginning to unremember

why I'd ever tried to quit: whom I was trying to live for, or impress, at the time.

"Honestly," I said into the darkness. "It's usually a whole lot harder."

Your mother shook her head—laterally, ambiguously—and poured some wine into her glass.

"Sammy and me," she said. "We used to be best pals."

"You *are* best pals!" I said. "And you're going to be even better pals, once we get this process down."

You were right about this, you know: I could be such a fucking phony.

Your mother held up her glass in a sort of toast to nothing. "I do appreciate what you've done for us," she said. "Even if I can never do it. You've still given him so much."

"He's given me a lot, too," I said—quickly, brightly, with the casual clarity of a firm but minimal affection. "You all have."

"But it still feels like shit, you know, watching you talk to him," she said. "It makes me feel the way I felt that first day I took him to the doctor and the guy looked at me like I'd broken Sammy's arm. I know that look because my mom actually did break my arm once."

"Jesus, Sandi."

"Like, how could you do something this awful to your own kid? How could you fail them so badly?"

"What you are doing now is the opposite of failing him," I said. "Being open to this technology. Trusting it. Letting me into your lives like this." It was embarrassing how much I meant this, but it still came out a little histrionic. "It's actually really brave, what you're doing."

Your mother shrugged and lit another cigarette. I'd somehow finished mine already.

"Brave," your mother said. "Yeah. Paying someone else to talk to your kid 'cause you still don't know how. Not even paying, actually, 'cause the state pays for you. Yeah, this is real mother-of-the-year-type stuff over here. Real United 93–type heroism."

It wasn't the state, per se—the Center had covered half my salary, before I decided to forgo that part—but this, I knew, would not have made your mother feel better. I hated that I couldn't make her believe the things I actually meant, and I wondered for the first time if this was how she felt when she spoke to you and found herself disappearing. I wondered if you missed her in those moments, or if you didn't know her well enough to. You really would have been best buds, I think, if you'd ever had the chance.

I reached out toward your mother, fingers arced in the universal request for a drag; our hands touched briefly as she handed me her cigarette.

"My husband died last year," I said.

Your mother stilled and looked at me. Under the porch light, I could see that her face had taken on some new lumpiness over the months. I wasn't sure if she was getting thinner or fatter. Something seemed to be changing, though, was the point.

"Yeah," she said. "I think I'd known that." She sounded sorry but not surprised, sad but not afraid to be; it was a tone not a lot of people could manage. "I mean, I had known, but I figured it was your own business."

She tilted the wine bottle toward me; I waved it away.

"What happened?" she asked.

I squinted at the stars. I didn't know any of them except Orion.

"It was an accident," I said. "With some pills."

"Oh," your mother said, and crossed herself. "I'm sorry."

I didn't know if she meant for the asking, or the crossing, or the thing itself.

"My daughter's afraid of her Flintstones vitamins now. She's afraid of a lot of things, these days." I thought of the bath mat. "He's been gone a year and a half and she's back to wetting the bed. Doing this thing with her hair that makes it look like she's got alopecia. And I have a *lot* of help from my mother." My mother, it was fairer to say, enjoyed some modest assistance from me. "I can't imagine doing what you've been doing all these years, Sandi. I never could have done it."

Your mother was quiet for a moment. I wondered if you were still awake above us. Too late, I thought to wonder whether you could hear this conversation.

"Well, you never really know what you can do," your mother said.

"Yes," I said. "I guess that's true."

I reached out for another drag, and your mother threw the pack into my lap. She fished in her pocket for the lighter, then threw that at me, too.

"The Choad Toad is still alive, naturally," she said. "Lives in Florida, has a new family. I looked him up on the web once, there was this picture of him with that big blue fish? You know, with the spiky things?"

I lit another cigarette. "A marlin."

"Yeah," she said. "Who knows why, but I think about that all the time."

I took a drag, and felt another lift of chemical optimism: so marginal, so modest, it seemed it must mean something real.

"Well, Sammy isn't going anywhere," I said. "And I'm not going anywhere, either. And when you think about it, Sandi"—and this I honestly believed—"we have all the time in the world."

"Sure," your mother said faintly.

Japanese has the words *koko*, for an object near the speaker, and *soko*, for an object near the listener. Then there's *asoko*, for an object far from both. Above us, I could feel your light go out.

"Why does that guy have all those plates in his yard?" I asked a while later.

"There used to be a cat that came by." Your mother blew some smoke over her shoulder, as though she'd already forgotten I didn't mind it. "It disappeared years ago, but he still tries to feed it."

"That's sad," I said.

"Raccoons and stuff eat it, though," she said. "Wouldn't it be sadder if he stopped?"

I wondered how many raccoons lived in the neighborhood. I tried to remember if I'd ever seen one.

"Yes," I said. "It would."

Chapter 15

IN PENANCE, I TOOK you on a whale watch.

This had been in the works for a while. "In honor of Chekhov!" I'd been exclaiming. *That was a shark*, you kept saying, as though I didn't know that already.

My first plan had been to take you to the aquarium. It's actually not a great aquarium—like everything in Boston, it's sort of stubbornly second-rate. I guess I wanted you to see the octopus. Maybe I wanted to see him again myself. But after the debacle of the Serious Conversation, I was glad a more substantive outing was in the books.

The morning of the whale watch, I pulled up to your house a few minutes early. I'd told your mother I'd be there for you at six. It was going to be spring tomorrow, from an astronomical standpoint, but the mornings were still dark and sour, damp in that weird way that has nothing to do with precipitation. It would be extremely cold on the ocean, and it was probably much too early in the season for whales; the tiny outfit that had sold me the tickets made absolutely zero promises in their literature. Still, I thought, it would be nice for us to be out on the water. Out anywhere, really. When your mother emerged with you at 5:57, I checked the impulse to ask if you'd be warm enough in your hat.

"Have fun," your mother said, collapsing your chair into my trunk. "You could not pay me to get on a boat at this hour."

We drove to Alewife in silence. I'd tried to scour the Cheez-It dust from the creases of the seats, but the vehicle still radiated an undeniable sense of having recently been occupied by a child. Which it had, and which you knew, of course—although we never talked about it, and obviously wouldn't be starting today. Today, for the first time in a long while, we wouldn't be talking about anything at all.

I will admit I'd been a bit concerned about the outing. I wondered how you'd manage on the T—the unfortunate jostling, the terrorizing fluorescence. But what worried me most was our not speaking: that it would feel too much like we'd regressed somehow, to a place before our own beginnings. But it didn't have to feel that way, I told myself now. I reminded myself of all the typical silences that comprise a typical relationship, all the silences in the world that mean absolutely nothing at all.

Beside me, you stared out the window, your head vibrating audibly against the glass.

I turned on the radio, but Top 40 was unlistenable—all smashing parts and male bellowing from inside what seemed to be tin cans. I flipped around to oldies; 103.3 was Billy Joel, and I looked at you and smiled. You'd once done a pretty funny medical history to the tune of "We Didn't Start the Fire"—*Prozac, Seroquel, progress at a standstill; Depakote, trazodone, bad news re: muscle tone; Valium, Ativan, smelly adult daycare van*—"Stop, stop," I'd said, laughing, but you didn't. *Anafranil, Benadryl, love is an acquired skill; Risperdal, Lamictal, who else do we have to call?* But it seemed you were not in the mood to reprise it now. There was a morning program on NPR—a lucid, hypercaffeinated discussion about some arcane point of foreign policy—but I hated not knowing what you thought of it, and, without knowing, did not know how to react to it myself.

At Alewife, we rode the elevator down to the subway. The station smelled like urine, which embarrassed me obscurely.

A while later, I said, "I've always wondered if the colors of the lines were supposed to mean something." We were on the Red Line still, approaching Charles/MGH. It was a challenge not to ask you questions, even ones you might conceivably answer. I didn't like to force you into pantomime; I knew you hated to express yourself in terms that couldn't do full justice to your thoughts. You would have been a hopeless student of foreign language, I often thought, before reminding myself you'd mastered something far more difficult than that.

"Like, Blue for water, Green for Boston Common, Red for, one supposes, Harvard?" I said. "I don't know what the Orange Line would be in this paradigm."

You said nothing, of course, which is about what this comment deserved. Still, I'm sure you would have mustered a suitably withering response, if you'd been talking. I wished I could have known what you'd have said.

We burst up and out of the tunnel. A sullen sunrise was beginning to leak out over the Charles, but most people on the train didn't bother to look.

We transferred at Park Street. The doors opened before us, releasing a steam of chestnut and humidity. I thumped your wheelchair along the platform. This gave me the same sick, hyperprotective feeling as maneuvering newborn JoJo in her stroller. I remembered how entirely ready I'd been to throw myself in front of a train for that child, how it seemed as though I'd been waiting my whole life to do exactly that. How I very nearly wished—in fact, perhaps I did!—that someone would give me half a reason to do it.

But as it was, none of that proved necessary, then or now. Around us: Red Sox hat, Red Sox hat, coeds in pajamas and full stage makeup. Little visored man with a pencil held out in front of him defensively. Tired-looking woman dragging a suitcase with a wonky wheel. We followed her to the Green Line, where she looked at the suitcase longingly: I could tell she wanted to sit on it. A thuggish-looking Celtics meathead glanced at us; I bent down to adjust your scarf. My hair brushed your face, and you moved toward or into it— whether intentionally or not, I cannot say—and this is when I spotted Tyruil, staring straight at us from across the tracks.

Languages differentiate between contact and vertical alignment, attachment and containment; they tend also to take special note of proximity. I stood up very straight and took several steps away from you.

I wondered how long Tyruil had been watching us—he had an odd, furtive little smile on his lips, although it is entirely possible he just walks around like that. I snapped my own expression closed—in doing so, I could feel how open, how entirely revealing it had been—and gave Tyruil a jaunty little wave. He responded with a sort of sideways two-finger salute: something like a flaccid peace sign. How I loathe the baby boomers.

Three especially loathsome facts about Tyruil in particular: 1) he always makes a whole big point of pronouncing the *h* in words like "when" or "whom" (and it is somehow *always* "whom" with him; I swear he contrives his sentences this way); 2) he is descended from a vast potato-chip fortune and is extremely sensitive about it; and 3) he conspired to get me kicked out of my program, which, if you'd talked to me a year ago, I would have said ruined my life. It didn't, actually, but Tyruil didn't know that, and I would never get to tell him. All of this galled me tremendously.

On the platform, I willed my face to remain neutral and still, drained of all lingering jubilation. Our trains pulled into the station more or less simultaneously, and I gave Tyruil another wave—this one apologetic, as though certainly we would have talked, and what a fine time we'd have had, if this conspiring of the fates had not prevented us. I could not see his reaction, and I didn't stop to try. Instead I hustled you through the doors with gestures of great urgency, although there turned out to be plenty of room on the train.

The trouble with Tyruil began on the second day of the Thirty-Seventh Annual Linguistics and Philosophy of Language Conference. In retrospect, I suppose we must have loathed each other before then, in that genteel way academics wish general ruination upon each other. But the real scandal erupted at the luncheon, immediately before the panel on which we'd both been invited to speak.

It was the kind of reception where you could tell they'd purposefully arranged food that would be really hard to steal. Cold cuts without bread, egg salad in mason jars, that sort of thing. A man in an actual bowtie was calling linguistic determinism imperialist—he was going on about Orientalism, the Clash of Civilizations, all that. He was from Yale, and I happened to know that his grandfather had personally orchestrated several of the more brutal campaigns of the Boer War.

"Oh, not *you*, too," Tyruil said, and rolled his eyes away from Bowtie.

I waited for him to say more, but this, it seemed, was the entirely of his rebuttal.

And so I spoke, noting that many of the early practitioners of linguistic determinism had actually wanted to prove that indigenous groups *were* sophisticated through a thorough investigation of their languages.

But instead of agreeing, Tyruil laughed right in my face; he said that I'd missed the point entirely. He had a disconcerting habit of looking at you intently while he was speaking, then looking away when you replied; most people do the opposite. The political implications of an idea, he said, had no bearing on its truth. His head now was pitched toward the egg salads, primly scooped into their little nests.

I said that I thought an idea's utility in the world had a great deal of bearing on whether it was a good idea in the first place.

"Then I think you belong in a different department," said Tyruil. Then he muttered: "Maybe a different sort of institution altogether."

He meant a mental hospital, I figured, though he later claimed he'd only meant a second-tier college.

"And I think you are being intellectually flatulent," I said. He laughed again and said, "I think you mean flaccid."

"No," I said severely. "I mean flatulent, precisely."

Tyruil looked at Bowtie and said, "I think someone here is very much in over her head," and this is when the wine was spilled. Some would later state that it was thrown. Languages often distinguish between causing and letting, between acting on something and enabling its exposure to a secondary force. In any event, Tyruil had to dash off to the bathroom and miss his part of the panel, where, by many accounts, I was a great triumph.

"Christ!" he said, immediately before fleeing. "Are you— is she sticking out her *tongue* at me?"

"No," I said. And then: "It's a nervous habit that I have."

I did write a letter of apology. At my mother's insistence, I also offered to pay for his dry cleaning. Tyruil wrote back that this would not be necessary, and that he'd quite forgotten the incident, as he was tremendously occupied with preparations for the publication of his fourth book. He added with some emphasis that he hoped I was taking care of myself, and he was sending all best wishes *for my health*.

I know I never told you any of this. On the train I only said, "That man is my nemesis."

You raised your eyebrow, requesting elaboration, but I pretended not to understand you. I suppose in part I was embarrassed. Not because the wine was spilled—an occurrence that, while not my doing, was just and also very funny—but because I didn't know how to tell the story all around it. "What happened?" my mother kept asking me afterward, and I led her to believe I felt the particulars would be beyond her comprehension. Really, they were beyond my own. Because I *agreed* with Tyruil, I thought at the time. And yet something about him telling me I was agreeing with him the wrong way made me want to disagree with him entirely. I don't know that I'd thought much about the utility question before the conference; in the offices and at the lecterns of academia, the question of the world does not come up. But I suppose even I could see that we were in some sense choosing what to believe in—when we picked our research areas, settled into our intellectual commitments, lovingly mapped the borders of the tiny fiefdoms we'd spend our whole careers defending. Surely what those beliefs *did* could come to be relevant in our choosing?

This seems extremely obvious to me now, of course, as it was that day on the T—my belief in you galloping alongside the train, propelling us up to the street, toward the water and the light.

We emerged into gray, friable clouds; postindustrial brick buildings glowing ruddy in the morning light. A bunch of fat-bottomed seagulls strutted around pompously. We were very near the water now, which is what makes Boston seem so much more than it is. I was suddenly feeling much better.

On the whale watch, we had choppy waters. Teeth-chattering wind, hyperventilic exhilaration. The sea smelled like everything they always say it does—salt and silt and blood and fish, all borne upon some wild kinetic energy. I clutched at the sleeve of your jacket.

"The Jahai of Malaysia have many words for smells," I shouted. "There's a word for rich carnivorous sanguinary smells, a word for prickly smoky acrid smells, and on and on." The sea surged, and I grabbed at the railing. "They are adept at identifying smells in testing. English speakers, with our comparatively limited vocabulary, prove hopeless."

You gave no indication of having heard me—which perhaps you hadn't, over the thrum and thrash of the motor, the sublingual expressions of awe all around us. We'd gotten a few looks by then—kindly, understanding ones, aggressively acknowledging the good deed I was doing—but mostly, people were not looking at us at all. Mostly, they were watching for the whales. You were very good at spotting them—differentiating the solidity of a patch of darkened sea from the emerging back of a living creature—whereas I thought I saw them everywhere: roil of hump, virgule of fin.

"There!" I'd say. Then: "There!" Then: "Oh, I guess . . . Oh, no. I guess not. No."

When a whale finally did breach beside us, the fact of it was unmistakable. A cry went up across the ship, and you gasped along with the rest of us. The whale crashed so close that sea-spray hit our faces; through all of it, you had not flinched. "You've got the nerve of a canal horse!" I shouted: a phrase inherited from my father, inherited from his ancient father. Not knowing what else to do, I swiped at you joyfully with my hat.

You leaned toward me, looking stricken and a little pale, and I did not care if anyone was watching.

Then you curled over the railing and vomited into the water.

I have been thinking lately about time.

In English, time is a distance. In Greek or Spanish, it's a shape or size. Aspect indicates how matters unfold within— along?—it. Events, we understand, have end points. States go on indefinitely.

The night of the whale watch, I realized there was some-thing bothering me about the Chekhov story.

That monologue you'd given about the ending, with its eternal, cosmic, out-of-time present tense—is that the mo-ment I fell in love with you? It certainly was one of them. But in Russian, I was remembering, tense is negotiable.

I wondered if I could find the original version.

I could.

I wondered if I could read it.

Just barely.

Only well enough, in fact, to ascertain one thing. That key shift that had so astonished you—it wasn't really there at all. All along, it was just a trick of the translation.

Chapter 16

"I WOULD LIKE YOU to take your daughter for ice cream," said my mother the next morning.

"What?" I said. I was still brooding over Chekhov. So what, I was asking myself: so what, so what. So a story's greatest grace turns out to be a flaw: something between an interpretation and an imposition. So we compound this distortion with every reading. We compound some new meaning, too, and this has to count for something. When you look at it a certain way, it counts for everything!

"Your daughter," my mother said. She was actually pointing. Outside, Jo was bouncing around the yard, making unconventional use of a carrot in the building of her snowman. Instead of serving as the snowman's nose, the carrot was made to stick out of his foot, then grow out of his head like a single, majestic horn. The obvious gag would never have occurred to her—my sweet, uncorrupted child.

"Ice cream?" I said. "Mom, it's *freezing*."

"You are entirely too wrapped up in that job," my mother said sharply. "And frankly, it's getting kind of weird."

At this, I felt something crackle, something fall, within me. An object in a fire settling into its own immolation.

"What do you mean?" I said. I spoke with what I hoped was a supremely impersonal curiosity.

"You are over there day and night," my mother said. "We hardly ever see you."

I could feel her refusing to glance at my left hand. She'd recently noticed that I'd taken off my wedding ring, though I don't think she'd decided yet whether this represented some big new policy. Because she'd been encouraging me for months to do this—lightly, therapeutically—she could ask nothing about it now.

"I know you're working more hours than you're getting paid for," she said. "And I'm glad you're passionate about this job—"

"I'm not *passionate* about it, good *God*," I said. Because this, really, was too much. "I am grateful for it, certainly. I'm committed to it, absolutely."

My mother handed me a plate and said, "It's just that I've never known you to allow yourself to be taken advantage of before."

I did not know how to respond to this remark. It seemed a dig on my general character—a truly good person would, it seemed, allow herself to be taken advantage of from time to time—so I wasn't sure I wanted to deny that this was what was happening now. And on another level, I must have been pleased that my mother had supplied such a sympathetic narrative: poor good-hearted Angela, devoted to her work so far beyond what her modest compensation would require! It seemed maybe we could leave the explanation there and let the circumstances grow around it, until the whole thing calcified into myth.

"And also," my mother said, "sometimes someone calls here."

At this, I sat back in my chair. "What?"

"There have been calls," she said. "Usually at night. The person just hangs up."

I stared into my plate. A smiling, ghoulish visage stared back at me; its eyes, perversely, were yellow raisins. I guess the whole thing was meant to be a pancake.

"Why didn't you say anything?" I asked.

"I thought it would stop. And I didn't want to worry you."

"Well, you have now."

"Well, maybe it's time for you to be a little worried." My mother tapped on the picture window with her spatula, summoning JoJo inside. "Sometimes, a little worry is healthy."

There was never any point in quibbling with my mother's notions about health.

"It's tough work you're doing," she said, shoveling a pancake onto JoJo's plate. This one's features, I noted with some relief, were comprised entirely of chocolate chips. "It can be all-consuming. I've had problem clients myself, you know. Over the years."

She tapped on the glass again. The carrot was growing out of the snowman's back now, as though somebody had stabbed him from behind.

"That's why boundaries are so important," my mother said.

"I'll take her for hot chocolate," I said, and ate the eyeball off my pancake.

*

And so we went to Burdick's, in Harvard Square. It was after four and not quite dark: the modest consolations of a New England spring. After a while, you'll take anything at all.

JoJo kicked at the slush, demanded a trip to the Curious George store.

"What's George so curious about anyway?" I asked.

"Everything."

"Just like you." I ruffled her hair. It was true she had developed a bit of a bald spot, which my mother had attempted to conceal with an enormous barrette. "Smart monkey."

"I'm not a monkey!"

"Since when?"

"Since ever!"

"You're so sure about that?"

It seemed I had her there.

Inside, we took a seat by the window. JoJo swung her legs and licked the whipped cream straight out of her mug. I scanned the faces in the square: no-nonsense academics, tired service workers grabbing sandwiches on their breaks. A couple of dreamy kids on college tours. I was looking for Tyruil, I realized. Maybe Fitzwilliams, though I had no reason to believe he'd ever once left the linguistics building. I'd certainly never personally observed him beyond it. A couple holding hands passed by: miniature dark-eyed girl, acned youth holding *Critique of Pure Reason* facing outward, hoping everyone would notice—and, goddammit, I had! An exhausted-looking mother shepherding a girl in bright red mittens. Should Josephine be wearing mittens? No, I decided. It was far too warm.

"Hey, JoJo, can I ask you a question?"

She nodded.

"Do you remember how you learned to talk?"

She frowned into her chocolate. She had a spot of whipped cream on her nose, which was too endearing to remove. She shook her head.

"Ah well," I said. "Shot in the dark."

My tea was getting cold already. I wasn't looking forward to the T, to rush hour, to navigating JoJo through the turnstiles and finding her a height-appropriate spot where she could hang on. She wasn't really the right size for public transportation. The T was always too hot, so we'd have to wrangle off the top part of her snowsuit, then wrangle it back on again in the station. Then the long walk home: JoJo jumping noisily into half-muddied snow drifts in other people's yards. The moon a stingy little squint above us. Too dark to even play I Spy.

"I think I always knew," she said.

"What? Oh, how to talk, you mean." Her bald spot was less obvious from this angle; kids her own size, I told myself, might not even notice it at all. "Well, if you did, you kept it a whole big secret for a while."

She licked her whipped cream again, more thoughtfully this time. "Maybe you taught me," she said.

"Nope."

"Maybe Daddy."

"Nah, not him either. Sorry, kiddo."

I was still studying the square, searching for faces I might know. I *wanted* Tyruil to happen by, I realized, to see me with my daughter. To see me out on another outing, one of many different outings I was prone to undertake with many different people, in my full and varied life. These were the kinds of lives people lived, outside the tower: they defied easy categorization. They had complexities and depths! They were, fundamentally, none of anyone else's business.

"Mommy. Mommy. Mom." Jo was tugging on my sweater, which meant something had just occurred to her. She had a tendency to take a thought's suddenness as an indication of its urgency. "Mom. Can we get a chocolate mouse?"

"I suppose we can."

"Could we get two?"

"I suppose we could."

"If we had three," she said, with flagrant slyness, "then we'd have three blind mice."

Such an extraordinary example of the perlocutionary speech act! They should teach that one in universities. I had the urge to kiss my daughter's bald spot, but I didn't want her to know I'd seen it.

Instead, I said, "What makes you think those mice are blind?"

"They're made of *chocolate*, Mommy." She sounded a little concerned, as though it was possible I hadn't known this.

"A fair point," I said. "Very well. Three blind mice it is."

And just like that, my child was extremely happy. Most of parenting is exactly as hard as they say it is. But a few things are just a little bit too easy.

Outside, in the square, a bunch of kids were marching

around, shouting about "No blood for oil!" I wondered who they thought they were talking to.

JoJo held my hand. "It's getting dark already," she observed.

I gave her mittenless fingers a little squeeze.

"Dark, kid," I told her. "With an *r.*"

Later, I found my mother sitting in front of the television.

"You gave her three chocolate mice?" she said when she saw me.

"She made a very strong case for herself."

"She'll be up all night, you realize."

My mother, I saw, looked absolutely distraught.

"I'm sorry," I said. "I *am*. Do you want help with the dishes, or something?"

"She'll be bouncing off the goddamn walls."

"I'll go read to her or something," I said. And then: "Have you been *crying?*"

She pointed at the television. "We're at war."

"We *are?*"

My mother gave a short, helpless squawk of a laugh.

In her room, JoJo was indeed crashing hard, staring bug-eyed at the ceiling. I sat at the end of her bed and stroked her foot.

"Doing all right, kid?" I said. I did feel bad about the chocolate.

"Can I tell you a secret?" she whispered. Her sheets were clutched up around her chin. The thing about things that seem too easy is that they just aren't finished yet—I'd learned that about a zillion times. And yet I struggled to behave as though I actually believed this. I was always thinking that maybe this time, maybe just this one time, I'd found a loophole.

"Of course," I said.

"Sometimes, I still miss Daddy."

"Oh, sweetheart." I began crawling into bed with her. "I know that, honey. I know. I know."

I stroked her hair, her forehead, her little palm.

"I'm awfully sorry, kid," I said. "It's been an absolutely rotten deal."

She made a sniffing sound, and I readied my soul for her crying. But it seemed that she was actually just sniffing.

"You smell like coffee," she said, wrinkling her nose.

"Ah. Well, I did have some before dinner."

"Can I have some tomorrow?"

"No." I knew the answer to this one. "Coffee is for grown-ups."

"That isn't fair."

"Think of it as one more thing to look forward to," I said, and sighed into her hair. She still used baby shampoo, though it could only be a matter of time before she came to view this as insulting. Literacy, I was sure, would bring with it all sorts of problems.

"Can you tell me something about Daddy?" said JoJo. "Something I don't know yet."

I considered this request.

"He never tied his shoelaces," I said. "Yet he somehow never tripped."

"But he knew how to tie them?"

"Yes," I said. "I am almost certain that he did."

"Oh," my daughter breathed.

I ran my hands through her hair, made some gestures toward braiding.

"It doesn't have to be a secret, you know," I said. "That you miss your dad."

"I know," JoJo said, and snuggled into my armpit.

"You don't have to keep any secrets from me, actually," I told her. "Unless later, for your own personal reasons, you should want to."

She murmured something into my torso.

"What's that?" I said, and she turned her head to look at me.

"I didn't want to make you sad," she said.

"Oh." I felt something in my center clench, some place I didn't know I had a muscle. "Well, that is not your purview."

"You used to cry a lot, though."

"That is true," I said. I'd forgotten. "But I'm not as sad anymore."

We lay like that for a while, until her breathing turned toward sleep.

"Good night, my *nattdet*," I said, as I was leaving.

"What does that mean, Mommy?"

"Whatever you want it to, kiddo," I said, and quietly closed the door.

*

"I meant to tell you earlier," said my mother, when I emerged from JoJo's bedroom. "There was another call when you were out."

She was standing in the kitchen, scrubbing furiously at one of our more hopeless pans. In the living room behind her, the TV was still blaring.

"It's probably just telemarketers," I said.

My mother looked at me with the same mystification I'd seen earlier—as though, after all this time and expensive education, it was possible that I was actually getting dumber.

"Telemarketers *want* to talk to you," she said. "That's the entire point."

"That pan's never going to get clean, you know," I said.

"It gets clean*er*."

"This stuff seems pretty bad," I said, gesturing toward the TV.

My mother turned off the tap and shook her head in a huffy, equine little way. "I have no idea where you've been this winter," she said. "But we need you to come back."

"I'm right here," I said, and we sat down together to watch the war.

"Someone's been calling me at home," I told you the next morning.

You dawdled for ten million minutes and then wrote, geriatrically:

How extraordinary.

The blinds in your little room were pulled halfway down,

making a dark morning even darker; your bed was disorderly, and not because we'd been up to anything. So you'd had a rough night too, I figured.

"Someone's been calling and hanging up, I mean."

Not another suitor, I hope.

"Do you think it could be your sister?"

I cannot think of why she'd do that, you wrote. This took eons: diadems dropped and doges surrendered. *Can you?*

I could, actually, think of a few paranoid reasons, but it seemed best not to bring them up now.

"Well, it's someone," I said instead.

You flicked your pointer finger in that little shrug-like motion that meant you had nothing else to add. I was familiar by now with this particular mood of yours—arid, oblique. Some endangered snow leopard licking its paws behind a rock on a mountain. Like the photographers had all the time in the world!

"Have you been feeling better?" I asked politely.

In what respect?

I gritted my teeth. "I'm sorry about the boat," I said. "I didn't know you got seasick."

I did not point out that it would have been impossible for me to know that, so it wasn't totally my fault.

The boat, she says, you wrote. *She is sorry about the boat. About the boat, she says, she is sorry.*

"You're being a real treat today."

And once again, my love, this is why you are being so handsomely compensated for your time.

You knew this wasn't my fault—that it was nobody's

fault, and there was nothing we could do about it at the moment. And yet the fact of my employment made both of us edgy, in our different ways. I didn't like to talk about it, while you kept trying to make jokes—jokes that never quite landed, which is how I knew you still hadn't found an angle, a way to tell yourself this part of our story.

"OK," I said. "You're angry at me. Fine. I wasn't thrilled with how that conversation went either, you know."

Not thrilled? you wrote. *Oh my God.*

"What?"

You're still doing it.

"Doing what?" I said, and shook your arm a little. "Doing *what?*"

Sam appreciates their support? you wrote. *It means so much to him?*

"Well, doesn't it?"

That isn't how I talk.

"They don't know how you talk."

At this, you slammed the table in a way that clearly meant *Exactly.*

"Well, what the hell was I supposed to do?" I said. "Would it have been better if I had done some kind of impression? Tried to capture your voice? Your little tics?"

You think you're the only one who sees other people? you wrote. *Because I know some things about you that you don't know.*

"Tried to make all your jokes for you? You know they wouldn't have been as good." Then I said: "Like what kinds of things?"

And I told you it would be like that, you wrote. *I told you I didn't want a scene!*

"Well, I don't know what to tell you," I said. "Real life has scenes. I think we're having one right now, in fact!"

I was digging into your arm a little too hard, I realized; I made a point of releasing my fingers one by one, like a pianist practicing a downward scale.

"I was being polite," I said. "I was trying to smooth things over."

You were being fake, you said. *And what you were trying to be was fake.*

"You think fake is the worst of our problems?" I said. "You made me look like a *fraud*. And did you ever consider that?"

I could almost hear your response to this—(*Dreadfully sorry to have been an embarrassment! That must have been positively hideous for you!*)—but instead, you said nothing. Your silence was the one thing that truly unsettled me in our arguments; I could never tell if it was the message, or the medium, that you were rejecting. But of course you knew this too.

Why was it I could speak with you the way I did—when others, it seemed, could not? It isn't that I haven't wondered. Was it because we loved each other—already, prelingually? Maybe. It might have just been that. But I realize this explanation is begging the question. And not in the colloquial way that normal people use that phrase, but in the devastating way philosophers do.

"It's not my fault it doesn't work with your mother," I said finally.

I'm certain you're not saying that it's mine.

"No," I said. The truth was, I did actually think you might have tried a little harder. But the rejoinder to this was so convincing, so fully formed in my mind—*you* hadn't tried? Who in this world had ever tried harder at anything than you?—that I was exhausted before I even began to mentally articulate it.

And I know you aren't asking me why I can't do a thing I cannot do, you said. *I assume you're not going to inquire what exactly it is about tap dancing that I find to be such a challenge.*

I pursed my lips and said, "I promise no one wants to see you tap dance."

You wiggled your toes—tap dancing, presumably—and I laughed, a little emptily. Your mother would be home from her shift soon. I wondered if I had previously been shouting.

"I'm sorry," I said. "I guess I haven't said that yet. I'm just—for one thing, I'm just extremely tired. Josephine had a bad night. She's sad about her father. She ate some mice she should not have. There's the war, of course." The light outside your window was changing character somehow: shifting in shape, if not exactly in color. I wanted to cry again, amazingly. "I've just been so worried lately."

It was true, I realized, although "worried" wasn't exactly the word. Instead I felt as though something terrible had already happened, and I'd forgotten it somehow; I kept scanning my memory to find out what it was and coming up with nothing. As though it was too awful to remember, and maybe I shouldn't even try. This was something like the inverse of those mornings after Peter died: the dumb blank moments right after waking, a blink of purely idiot time, before the smash of memory.

You leaned forward, and I bent myself to follow you.

Quit worrying, you said. *Worrying is pointless.*

"Well, a lot of things are pointless, and people do them anyway."

Worried is just a feeling.

"Pretty much *everything* is just a feeling," I said. "Love is just a feeling!"

Love is a reality. Worried is—you paused—*an interpretation.*

"I don't know about that," I said. "I think they're probably both just feelings. Cognitive distortions, most likely."

You hated those.

Fine, you said. *So say worried is a feeling. Is it the biggest one in the room right now?*

I couldn't bear to think what kind of group therapy session you must be quoting at me here; I'd thought we'd moved well beyond the era of scripts and protocols and slogans.

"No," I said.

No, you wrote, and I could tell you meant it softly.

"No," I said again. "Of course not."

But what I really meant was: No. Not yet.

And anyway, you wrote, *whatever happens, we are still the two luckiest people in the world.*

"That's what the illusionist said to the fortune teller, and look what happened to them," I said. "Also, do not quote your own book at people! That is extremely obnoxious."

First of all, if anyone's quoting anyone, my book is quoting me, you said. *And also, the book isn't finished yet.*

"You're telling me they do escape, in the end?" I said. Such cheap plotting seemed beneath you. "I don't believe it."

Your eyes cut to somewhere beyond me, your gaze retreating to that place it lived before I really knew you.

I'm not saying they'll escape, you said. *I'm saying it isn't yet decided.*

In Russian—in many languages—possession is expressed not with a verb but a subject. Something less like "I have it" and something more like "it is on me." To an English speaker, this makes the act of having sound strangely passive: as though the thing in your possession could, at any moment, get up and walk away.

But think about it a little, and this is true of most things.

Think about it a little longer, and it's true of everything, in the end.

Chapter 17

THE OTHER SHOE DROPPED on a Tuesday morning, in a screwy, undignified little scene. One imagines ruination descending with a sort of stately dignity, but most of the time it just looks like everything else: half-baked and a little trite, with some canned dialogue and a bunch of random details that add up to nothing. You can remember these details for the rest of your life—in all likelihood, you will—and still, they'll never mean a goddamned thing.

It is some consolation to me now that we were no longer fighting. We had been, only moments earlier, even as we fucked. We were saying, wordlessly, *I am angry* and we were saying *I am sorry* and

I am sorry I am angry

I am sorry you are angry

I'm not sorry

I'm not angry well I was but now I'm not.

And I love you—

yes I KNOW that—

and I'm scared that—

don't you SAY that—

but I'm not saying anything—

yes you are and I can hear.

If you ask a linguist if something is a dialect or a language, they will always tell you: yes.

Strangely, I sometimes wish that we'd been caught a little

sooner. At least then, your family would have understood not just the category of the act, but also something of its character. They would have still been shocked, of course—repulsed, no doubt, confused both morally and logistically—but there would have been no question that they were seeing something real. It's just possible this might have convinced them. And if it hadn't, then their memory of that moment would have come to take the shape of our defiance—vengeance, even, as the years went on and on. They'd have seen what something true could look like—and, in disbelieving, destroyed it. This is the kind of thing that comes with very specific punishments in certain theologies.

But as it was, we were caught in no great state of grace. And it's these final moments we are doomed to recall with perfect clarity; everything else will recede at the normal pace of loss. And so here we are, forever: me half-crouched in a little hunch, underwear bunched awkwardly in my hands, you lying limply on the bed beside me, waiting for my help taking off the condom. Even I can see how much I must have looked like a criminal.

When the light in the room changed, you made a cry. A basic principle of linguistics is the arbitrary relationship between meaning and sound. My eyes flew to the door.

"Oh my God," said your sister. "Oh, my God."

"No," your mother was saying, simultaneously. "No, no, no, please no."

"Oh shit, oh shit," said Moira. "Get out of here! Get away from him!"

"No," said your mother. "No, no, no, no, no."

She seemed to be addressing someone. God, I later figured.

I had joined your mother in the chorus of "nos" by then—"No, it isn't what it looks like; no, it is, but we can explain; no, but we're in love; no, but we were going to tell you"—this last the only lie: it just came out.

"Take your clothes!" screamed your sister. "I mean— fuck!—put them *on* at least. Jesus Christ, I cannot believe what I'm seeing."

"No, I didn't mean that no I would not get my clothes; no, of course I'll get my clothes, and if you could give us just a minute to—; no, of course I understand that; no, I'm going, I'm going—no, see? I'm not touching him at all; no please, oh please, don't call the cops; no but see my shirt is on now, my hands are in the air; no, you just have to listen; no, I understand that *I* have to listen; no, I will listen, I will do nothing but listen; no, I definitely will stop talking, no, here—you see?—I've stopped."

I stopped. We all did. And then we seemed to turn toward you, as if waiting for a verdict. But in your eyes, I saw, was something like the end of language. And of course you said nothing at all.

I have been thinking lately about the future. Many languages don't express the future tense at all; some merely distinguish between events taking place now from those that are not. This latter category comprises the generic, the hypothetical, and the yet to come. *Realis* vs. *irrealis* is what they call that distinction.

The upside of this paradigm is the sheer magnitude of aspects in which we are together. The heft of considering them all at once. The downside is the puniness of that melting iceberg we call reality, and the terrifying solitude of any sucker still left there.

"What do we do if they find out?" I'd asked you once.

You didn't hesitate. You said: *We explain.*

And so, God help us, we did try.

We sat in your little yellow kitchen: you, your mother, and I. Moira stood at the window, hovering hawkishly. Her narrow face, I saw, was very pale.

"Let me explain," I said. And then: "We can explain."

Your sister was shifting her weight in odd contortions: standing on one foot, then the other; holding one arm across her body, then the other. Your mother was entirely still: too stunned, I think, not to listen.

"I can tell you what happened," I said. "But I think you should hear it from him."

Moira scoffed: an ugly, phlegmy sound in the back of her throat.

"I don't want you touching him," said your mother.

"I understand that," I said, and waited a respectful moment. The light coming in through the window was metallic, hitting the yellow Formica in a way that felt somehow sickening. "But if I don't touch him, then he can't talk."

"Well, isn't *that* convenient," said Moira.

"What are you talking about?" I said.

"Stop," your mother said. "Just stop."

I rubbed my eyes violently.

"I need to get the device," I said.

"You need to stay right where you are," said your mother.

I shut my eyes and squeezed them tight. Little pindots of light sparked within the darkness. Even with my eyes closed, I could feel that you'd gone quiet: your juddering, omnipresent energy seemed to somehow have short-circuited, leaving a stillness that was not calm but broken.

"Moira, get the damn thing," your mother said.

And so Moira went, returning with the device a minute later. She was actually pretty careful with it, and I must have taken this as a good sign: the fact that she was not yet willing to destroy your single means of communication. In retrospect, I wonder if she wasn't just mindful of preserving evidence. She was absolutely the kind of person who could think that way, that far ahead.

She placed the device on the table. Your mother stared at it as though it might start to generate words spontaneously. We all said nothing for a moment.

"Well?" I said. "May I?"

I hated asking permission like that, as though you were an object, or a woman at almost any point in history and in certain places still today. Your mother gave a hopeless, cornered little nod: permission to amputate a gangrenous limb.

I moved cautiously behind you. You smelled salty, a little oceanic—like me, I realized. I watched your shoulders rise and fall with your breathing. For the first time in our time together, I felt afraid to touch you.

"No point in being chivalrous now," said Moira—and really, she was right.

I placed my hand on yours. It seemed extremely important that I not exist in this moment. I willed myself to become an instrument: autonomic, agnostic, with no opinion on the future or the past.

Your hand began to move. Your sister stared in something like revulsion, as though watching a dead thing come to life. I willed myself to become an unperson; I willed you to understand why.

I started this, you wrote.

I looked up and said, "He didn't."

Don't interrupt me! Your hands were shaking slightly. I wanted to hold them, to kiss them. Instead, I hovered clinically. *I started this,* you said. *I did. I was only flirting with her at first because I was bored. And I wanted to throw her off a little.* You cut your eyes toward me. *I'm sorry.*

"That's OK," I said.

"Please shut up," said Moira politely. "You are not a part of this conversation."

But then—something changed. We—"connected" sounds stupid. But we saw each other somehow.

"Yes," said Moira. "You've clearly seen a lot of each other."

I know this is hard for you guys, you said. *I know it's a shock.*

"I cannot listen to this," said Moira.

Really? Your hand was moving quickly now, though when you were angry with me, you always seemed to type much slower. I guess you trusted that, no matter what, I would wait to find out what you'd say. *After 28 years, you can't listen to me for five minutes?*

"That isn't what she means," said your mother.

I'm sure it'd be easier if I wasn't talking at all, right? Then you wouldn't have to deal with me being a person, or wanting things—

"Honey, that's not what we—"

"Stop talking to that thing like he's in there!" shouted Moira. "You know you're just talking to her!"

Your mother was beginning to cry now, finally.

"That isn't true," I said.

"It's her," said Moira. "It's always just been—her. I'm sorry, Mom. I'm sorry, Sammy. But this whole thing is bullshit."

You slammed your hands on the table then, and something popped off the keyboard. The S key would have been poignant, but it was only #. We never used that one. Still, I dropped to the floor and began hunting, as though something extremely precious had been lost.

"You don't know that for sure," I heard your mother say above me.

"It's always just been bullshit," said Moira. "And at first I thought, well, how much harm could it do? Jesus Christ, I couldn't have imagined."

I abandoned my search for the # key, hitting my head on the table on the way up. We'd find it later, I told myself. We'd have plenty of time.

"That isn't true," I said, emerging. Your mother's face had grown splotchy from her crying. "Sandi. You know that isn't true."

"She knows that isn't true, huh?" said Moira. "Well, how does she know? Did you ever bother to prove it to her?"

"There've been entire conversations!" I said. "She's seen them. You've seen them. He wrote a whole paper!"

"You wrote it," said Moira. "You wrote that paper, and you wrote those conversations, and you never even bothered to try to convince us you didn't. You didn't need to. Because she wanted to believe you so badly."

Fuck you, Moira, you said.

"See, Mom? She's getting abusive. We honestly should call the police."

"We'll prove it," I said, looking at you desperately.

No, you wrote.

"We'll prove it to you."

No, we are not going to do that.

"What do you want us to do? We'll—I'll—do anything."

Moira glanced at your mother. She was staring intently at you, as if your face could somehow solve this thing.

"Then let's ask him a question you don't know the answer to," said Moira. She was speaking directly to me now. "No more chitchatting, no more what's a fish and what's your name or what did you think of this article in the fucking *New York Times.* No more tell me again how pretty I am, or whatever you're making him say to you when you're alone. Mom, you know, there's a good chance she is actually crazy."

Your mother had stopped crying by now. The splotchiness seemed to be migrating down her body, like blood poisoning.

"OK," I said. "We can do that. We can ask a question. Whatever you want."

"OK," said Moira. "Mom? What do you want to ask him? Something you're really, really sure she wouldn't know."

Your mother's eyes grew wide and spun around the room. I thought of all the big and terrible things I would want to ask you, if I were her: "Did I fail you? Did I know you? Can I still?" I wondered if she'd ever really wanted to ask those questions; I wondered if, even with all the practice and privacy in the world, she ever would.

Your mother's eyes seemed to settle. She looked right at you.

"What was your grandmother's favorite thing?" she asked.

I am not doing this, you said.

"Sam, please," I said.

I am not going to perform some party trick to convince my own mother I'm a human being.

"Even his principles are convenient!" said Moira. "Nice."

"Sam, *please,* just answer," I said, though I knew absolutely that you were not going to.

"See, Mom? Mom, you see? I'm sorry, but there just isn't—"

"It was the cuckoo clock," I said, and they both looked at me.

"What did you say?" said your mother.

"The clock," I said, pointing wildly. "That was his grandmother's favorite thing."

Your mother's face was breaking in a new way now. It was like a building that has sustained some fatal blow to its fundamental integrity, before it collapses entirely into dust.

"Did he tell you that?" she whispered.

"Yes," I said. "He won't say it now, but he did, he did tell me."

Moira made a little gagging motion with her throat; she reminded me of a cat coughing up a hairball. "Mom, *you* must have told her that," she said.

"I know I didn't tell her," said Sandi.

"Mom, you're forgetting."

"Moira, goddammit, this is the *one* thing I *know* right now. Don't tell me I don't know it."

Your mother was breathing a little crazily now—making clotted, glutinous sounds. All the cigarettes, I supposed.

"Then she guessed," said Moira. "She guessed. Mom, it's right there on the wall."

"I guessed? Sandi, come on." I looked straight at your mother, in a way I hoped was a little bullying. "Doesn't that seem just a bit far-fetched?"

"That is the least far-fetched explanation," said Moira. "You guessed. Mom, she guessed."

"I don't know," said your mother hoarsely. "I need to lie down. I need you to leave."

"Yes," I said. "I can leave. We can talk more later. You can ask more questions, if you want."

I wanted to say, we've been through a lot, you and me, and we will get through this thing, too. But I didn't want to provoke Moira, arousing her petty territorialism even further.

"I'll go now," I said, and patted your mother's hand. Moira regarded me with naked disgust. I felt tired in a disgusting, post-anesthesia sort of way. "We'll be in touch."

I stood and turned to you. You seemed to have absented yourself somehow: just left the room entirely, without ever moving a muscle. I did not know what to say. The problem wasn't that I couldn't tell you how I felt—I never really needed to, and didn't now. The problem was that no matter what I said, you could not reply; you could not tell me it was bullshit, if it was. Anything I said would be a proclamation you had to endure: a PSA, a highway billboard. Some lady showing you the alphabet, her cloying patience leaking all over everything, when you'd already written an entire novel in your head.

The only thing to say now, I decided, was something that did not invite a rejoinder. One of those last things people say to each other, until they say things again.

"I'll see you soon," I said finally.

"Don't be so sure," said Moira.

"I need you to be quiet, Moira," said your mother. "And, Angela, I need you to leave."

"I'm leaving."

"Make sure she has all her stuff, Mom. I don't want her pretending she has some excuse to come back here."

I turned and said, "I know we don't know each other well, Moira, but that is not the kind of maneuver I would ever think would work."

"You thought fucking a disabled child in his mother's own home would work," said Moira. "Just because you're a psychopath doesn't mean you're not stupid."

We are blind when we think we are invisible. I found I'd taken a few steps back, involuntarily.

"Why are you still talking?" said your mother. "Please be quiet. Please, oh please, just go."

"I'm going," I said. "I'm going."

And I went.

Outside, the sky was that flat white light that feels like it could be any time of day. Teens massed in front of the 7-Eleven. Their lunch break, I guessed, so maybe it was noon. I held my breath when I passed them, though of course they didn't look at me. Random woman pushing thirty: a color they have no name for.

We are blind when we think we are invisible—why did that sound so familiar? Something you said. Or maybe something I did. It bothered me I couldn't remember.

I could not go home yet. I didn't know where I would go instead. I decided to walk until I found out. I walked and walked, the morning playing on a loop that spiraled into ever-smaller circles, until the only thing remaining was your sister's chant ringing in my ears: "She guessed, she guessed, you guessed, she guessed."

And here's the hell of it: she was right. I did.

Chapter 18

I HAVE NOT BEEN entirely forthcoming. There are a few things I never told you.

My Chekhov discovery, for one. Your interpretation of the story was so lovely that I could not help but think that it was, in some profound way, correct. That it was truer than the details of words or translation—that you'd found something deeper, and its exact mechanics were beside the point.

Nevertheless, I should have told you. I realize you are entirely capable of handling disappointment.

So here's something else I never mentioned, in all my cooing about Basque and outlying languages and their particular secret magic, and our own. The Finno-Ulric language group is comprised of Hungarian, Finnish, and Estonian. These are unrelated to the other languages of the continent. The nations in which they are spoken have the highest suicide rates in Europe.

And I know we never really talked about my husband. I suppose this must have left you wondering some things. I can't imagine you didn't ask yourself if my love for you wasn't just a grief-induced hallucination. And of course I wondered if yours was only a projection—a form of gratitude, or dependency, or need. Anyone looking in from the outside would say these things were obvious; I would have said so too, probably, if I'd still been among them.

Anything we might have said to counter these ideas

would have sounded unpersuasive. Some truths can only be degraded by language; I've listened to my own courtroom testimony enough to know. I'm glad we never did this to each other—that we left certain things in that silence where we first met, and recognized each other, and to which we've now, both of us, returned.

I decided I would stay away for a while.

Our situation was difficult for your family to get used to; I understood that. My family wasn't going to be thrilled about it either—although I could see my mother enjoying dissecting the perversity of it all with Alan behind closed doors. Josephine, I imagined, would mostly just be disappointed that you weren't her father—although then again, she might be young enough, the future before us long enough, that perhaps one day, in a certain sense, you would be. But here, I knew, I was getting ahead of myself.

The bottom line, I told myself, was that your mother loved you and was grateful to have you back. In the end, she wouldn't want to stand in the way of the first meaningful desire you'd ever expressed. The only thing you'd ever been able to say you wanted. It wasn't what she wanted, no, but that's the whole thing about other people's freedom. You don't get to decide what to do with it. She'd realize this, just as soon as she'd had some time to think it over.

I figured a week would be reasonable.

And so I spent seven days not calling, not going to your house. During the days, I kept to my usual schedule—leaving just before 8, returning at 5:37 or 6:15, to maintain the irregularity of reality. I spent afternoons in the more literary of the non-Harvard squares—Davis, Porter, Central—lingering in bookstores and watching undergraduates shriek-flirt over aseasonal ice cream. I couldn't decide whether I wished to encourage or warn them; I think I wound up just creeping them out.

Josephine seemed to find my presence at her bath time troubling. She was very into schedules and personnel assignments and did not like disruptions to the routine. But my mother was happy, at first, to have me home in the evenings.

"It's really good to have you here," she said to me on night six.

"I'm so pleased to be prioritizing my family!" I exclaimed.

After seven days of not calling, I spent the next ten calling obsessively. There were straight-to-voicemails, hang ups, a couple of times when someone answered and seemed to wait for me to say something, although they never spoke. This could conceivably have been you, I understood, but I did not let myself dwell on the idea. Not knowing if you were really there, there was absolutely nothing I could say.

I was not overly deterred by your family's evasions. They seemed to me to be part of some necessary ritual: your mother's expression of real disapproval, my demonstration of true commitment and contrition. I deserved to be ignored for one week, two weeks—six! But eventually, I knew, your mother was going to want to talk to me.

And on this point, at least, I was right. Your mother picked up on the second day of the third week—this time, on the very first ring.

"Sandi," I said, before she even said hello. I somehow knew that it was her. I was getting a little psychic about the goings-on in your household—although not, I had to admit, when it had mattered most of all.

"Angie," your mother said. She sounded more marveling than embittered, which is how I understood she was alone.

"I'm listening," I said. I was standing in my childhood bedroom, phone cord twisted around my wrist. The flowered, existentially distressing wallpaper had been painted over long ago.

"I should have known you were too good to be true," your mother said at last.

I laughed and said, "I don't think anyone has ever accused me of *that* before."

"I don't think you're an evil person," she said, and I was very sorry I'd brought up the question of my essential nature. "Moira thinks you are. She thinks you're terrible."

"I'm sorry to hear that," I said, trying to sound a little sorrier than I actually was. Because some people are just going to be wrong about you. Moira seemed like someone whose good opinion I could live without.

"She says you see us all as lab rats."

"I absolutely don't."

"She says you're treating this whole thing as some experiment. Can he learn to talk? Can he learn to, to *fuck?*" Your mother made a sound somewhere between a choke and a chortle, though probably it was neither. "She says you're gonna take him on some talk show."

"What?" I said. "No. None of that is true. Sandi, listen to me."

And I could tell she actually was. In the background, I heard the faint sound of a laugh track.

"Sandi. He was in there all along. OK? He was. I know you know that." I was whispering now, hoping my mother wouldn't notice the cord snaking away from the living room. This probably should have reminded me of high school, but I never made unauthorized calls back then. "And he's—he's wonderful," I said. "He's smart and funny and profound and, and tough." I hated myself for this: this pleading accretion of adjectives. "Un-self-pitying, I mean. You raised a wonderful, wonderful person, and he was in there all along. And of course I didn't mean for this to happen. But can't you see how it could?"

"I don't know," said your mother. "I really—I just don't."

"Sandi, I know it's—I realize it's very weird," I said. "But he's, you know, he's almost thirty. This was going to happen sooner or later."

"No, it would not have," she said sharply. "If you hadn't come around, then none of this would have happened."

The laugh track rippled again in the space behind your mother. Syndication, at this late hour; a lot of those laughing people were probably dead.

"What I mean is," I said, "as soon as he could communicate, he was going to start making his own decisions."

"But that's the thing. I don't know if these are his decisions."

"What?" I said. And then, a moment later: "Sandi, *what?*"

She didn't answer me. And this, maybe, is when I first got scared. I'd believed your mother would come around not only because she loved you, but because she absolutely understood that you existed. It's true she didn't always know how to act that way—those anxious asking-for-a-bank-loan-type conversations, case in point. But I'd never doubted she would learn. I'd never doubted she believed you were a person, someone worth knowing and trying to know. And that any messiness that came along with that—any pain or confusion or unexpected complications, such as the one presently under discussion—well, that was worth it, too.

"But, Sandi, these *are* his decisions," I said. I was aware of speaking very gently. "And actually, you *do* know that. He explained it to you himself, remember?"

"God, you really think we're all just idiots, don't you?"

"What?"

"This is what Moira keeps telling me, and I hate that she keeps being right."

"Sandi, I have truly no idea what you're talking about."

"I *know* about the research paper," your mother said darkly.

"What?" I said again, although of course this time I knew exactly what.

"I know how they had to take it back and all."

"Oh, Christ—Leana's paper?" I flapped my arm in the direction of the living room, as though this was all Alan's fault somehow. As though if your mother could only know that, she would see how inconsequential it made everything else. "Is that what this is all about?"

"I know they wrote about it in the *Globe*," she said.

"Sandi. Come on. Some paper? Who cares?" I didn't like how frantic my own voice sounded. "Are you really gonna let a typo in some paper about some other kid entirely tell you you didn't see what you saw with your own eyes?"

"Oh, I know what I saw with my own eyes, all right."

I was aware of making some basic errors here.

"Sandi," I said. "Did you even read that paper? Because I didn't."

This was a lie: I'd read the paper, and the *Globe* article, too, several times. You could tell that the *Globe* people just loved getting to tack a sad, cynical little epilogue to the end of Leana's story—her beautiful account of the work she'd done with Nelly, their incredible achievements together. It wasn't that I doubted the reporting, exactly; Leana, it seemed, had indeed made some mistakes. But there was a grandiosity about the article that bugged me—as though the reporters, still high on the priest thing, imagined they'd found another massive scandal, instead of a single well-intentioned woman who turned out not to be so great at her job.

"Because I don't have *time* for that stuff anymore," I said to Sandi now. "Because I only care about what works. And you know this works. You've *seen* this work. I don't know what you think is in that paper, but it doesn't have anything to do with us." I was aware of trying to bleach the lunacy from my voice. "Frankly, I don't know where you even found it."

There was a silence then, and that silence seemed to pulse. I had the impression your mother felt she had made a mistake somehow, and was deciding what to do about it. I pictured you up in your room, waiting along with me.

"I've got to go," she said, and hung up the phone.

*

And so I stayed away, again, for even longer.

I took JoJo to the Children's Museum and to the swan boats. I took her to the playground and watched her chase the birds with a lunging, carnivorous intensity. Her father liked to chase birds, too, even well into his twenties—he said it was the only kind of fun a bird could have—but I didn't have the energy to tell her that just then.

My mother insisted on taking all of us to a protest in Copley Square.

"She won't understand what's going on," I said.

"She'll understand that something's going on," my mother said. "And that the adults around her are paying attention."

In the evenings, I helped my mother prepare our dinners. In spite of my pro bono work, our finances had been looking up that year; we ate veggie burgers and zucchini noodles and skipped the spaghetti, for a while. Easter was observed with special decadence; in JoJo's basket crouched six chocolate mice, to be held in escrow by my mother and dispensed on an appropriate schedule. My daughter hadn't gotten used to having me around so much, exactly, but she'd gotten used to being unsurprised by my presence. In the end, she'd gotten used to having no opinion about it.

I tried to think not of you but around you. I imagined what you might be seeing, might be reading—I couldn't stand to think they might not be letting you read. In the mornings, I thought of the blue slanted light angling through your curtains; the aquarium's reflection on the carpet outside your room. The flick of refracted neon when a fish turned abruptly away from the glass. Yellow sun. Orange orange. Blue fish.

My mother seemed to know something was wrong with me, but she couldn't figure out exactly what. Because here I was, finally doing what she wanted, humbly acknowledging that she'd been right—oh, so thunderously right!—all along. At her insistence, I'd even gone on dates with two perfectly appropriate men: one of them touched my breast in a taxicab, and the other one even called. (Wartime measures: I hope you'll forgive me.) Eventually, my mother seemed to resign herself to the idea that this was simply how it was with grown-up daughters. One always had one's suspicions.

I was trying very hard to stay away from language. But this, it turns out, cannot be avoided. Although it might not be the only way to think, it is the only one that I can manage. I know for sure because I've tried to stop.

At the beginning of the seventh week, your mother called.

"You're so sure he's in there," she said. "But how do you *know?*"

I was extremely prepared to answer this question.

"He talks," I said. "He reads. You've *seen* him read."

"Moira says I've seen him stare."

"That's what reading looks like!" I said, and took a breath. "He makes jokes. He writes papers. He writes papers about *Chekhov.*" Although I wasn't sure you'd actually finished it. "He does everything a human mind does. He does a whole lot more than most."

"I know why it seems like he's there," your mother said. I wondered if she was calling from the kitchen or the hall. I hoped wherever she was, you couldn't hear her. "But how do you know for sure? I mean, for absolutely certain."

"I don't," I told her reasonably. "I mean, how do I know for sure that *you're* there? Sandi, *philosophy* doesn't have an answer for this."

"I'm not talking about philosophy."

"But actually, you are." I was trying to sound scholarly but not pedantic. I wanted only to issue the subtlest reminder that on this subject, I was something like an expert, despite not having formally attained a terminal degree in my field. "I mean, how do you know anyone has a mind? That Moira does? That I do?"

"That's different."

"Why is it different? Because we talk out loud? That doesn't prove anything. Just because I talk doesn't mean *for sure* I'm not a robot. Or a computer program. Or a hallucination that you're having."

"That would certainly solve a lot of things," your mother said.

I could see I was losing her with this stuff.

"Sandi, let me ask you a question, OK?" I said. "How did you know I smoked?"

I could tell from her silence that this wasn't the question she'd been expecting. And so I waited, penitent and patient and with all the time in the world.

"You told me, didn't you?" she said at last.

"No," I said shyly. "I didn't. Because I never wanted you to know."

Vulnerability, affinity, shared stigmatized class-based vices: I'd thought through all of this ahead of time. I am not naturally conniving, but I can really throw myself into it in an emergency.

"But I smoke too," your mother said.

"I know that," I said. "But for some reason I was embarrassed anyway. I think I just got so used to hiding it. You know, in school and all."

Your mother sighed. "People do love to have an opinion."

"Which is why I'm very sure I didn't tell you," I said. "So how did you know?"

There was a pause. This made me jubilant with hope. The fact that your mother was actually thinking about this question meant she was still willing to be persuaded—as of course she must have wanted to be, so desperately. Playing to confirmation bias is a cheap maneuver, the sort of thing to be disdained in an academic argument, or at a certain sort of cocktail party. But these are the vanities of worlds where nothing really matters, where the stakes of ideas are always just other ideas. In this conversation, in a very real way, I was trying to save your life.

"I don't know," your mother said. "I guess I just knew."

"You just knew," I said. "Because sometimes people just know things. I—"

I stopped and shook myself. I'd been about to mention my premonition about the cuckoo clock—which would be a suicidal lunacy, even if it was actually a pretty good example of what I was talking about.

"Sandi," I said. "I know you've got a lot to think about. But what worries me is this. What if you're wrong? I mean, what if you're *wrong*. Can you imagine how bored he must be? How lonely? How scared? If you think there's even the slightest *chance* he's really in there, don't you think you should provide him with some sort of stimulation? Just in case?"

Your mother said nothing. I forced myself to tolerate ten solid seconds of her silence. In the living room behind me, I could hear JoJo doing some sort of expensive indoor hopscotch—the kind advertised relentlessly on Saturday mornings, ER bill not included.

"I would be happy to come by and do some exercises," I said. "Some reading. Maybe help with his paper. No conversation beyond that. You can supervise."

Your mother sighed then. It was a strange sigh, long and hissing, like an air mattress deflating very slowly, and when she spoke again, she did sound drained of something that had filled her for a good long time.

"I can't do that, Angie," she said. And then: "I don't think you really understand what's happening here."

I was too scared to ask what I did not understand; I was sure that whatever it was, I did not want to.

"You know," your mother said, "in all my wildest fears, I never, never dreamed this would happen. I had absolutely no idea."

"You didn't?" Through the phone I could hear a tapping, a faint whisk of fire. Something was dawning on me, finally. "Then why'd you come into the room that day?"

For that, clearly, was an ambush. I suppose I'd assumed your mother knew, or wondered, and in spite of our precautions, this hadn't surprised me all that much. Love is an extremely loud emotion: one always sort of suspects that everyone else in the room can hear it.

"Sandi?" I said. "How did you know?"

"How did I know? What the fuck does that matter? Someone saw you, made a guess, made a call. And guess what, they were right. Because sometimes people just know things, like you said."

She was speaking with some nastiness now.

"Someone saw us?" I flashed to a nauseating still of Moira crouched outside our bedroom. Then I got it. "You mean—Tyruil?" I said. "Tyruil, on the T?"

The image of Moira dissolved to Tyruil and his smug little face. I imagined him sitting in an office among snifters and scepters, the head of some large game animal behind him. Dialing, for some reason, a rotary phone. "It gives me no pleasure to make this call," he'd say, starting with the biggest lie first. He'd go on to talk lugubriously of duty and concern, though he didn't give a shit about anyone who couldn't give him more than he had already, and especially not people like your mother. During the 2000 election, he'd more or less admitted he didn't think poor people should be allowed to vote.

"Sandi, that is awful," I said. "Tyruil is *awful.*"

"I don't care if he's Osama bin Laden," your mother said. "He was right about you."

"He got me kicked out of my university."

Although that had been easy; this, I was realizing, must have taken some initiative, as well as a few little chores— casual conversation with Fitzwilliams about my whereabouts, brief phone call to the Center's chipper, non-HIPAA-bound receptionist—of the sort I would have assumed Tyruil would think were quite beneath him. I wondered if he'd gotten a re- search assistant involved somehow.

"So what?" your mother said. "That just means he was right about you from the start."

"What did he say we were doing?" I said. "Sandi, what on earth could we have been doing on the *subway* that could warrant ruining all our lives like this?"

"The subway? What are you even saying? Do you forget who you're talking to? Or do you always just pretend you're talking to no one?" Your mother, at last, was shouting at me. You'd hear her now, no matter where she was in the house. "It doesn't matter what happened on the fucking T! What matters is what I saw you doing to my son in my own home. Remember *that*? That is the conversation we are having."

"OK."

"No," she said. "I mean, it *was* the conversation. But now that conversation is over."

She made a husky, harrowing sound: the borderline grunt of the tennis player or the butter churner or any woman anywhere working far beyond her endurance.

"That's actually why I called," she said. "To tell you that."

*

I called your mother, she didn't answer. I called your sister, she told me to go fuck myself. I drove slowly by your house. There were grocery circulars all over your front stoop; I vowed to pick them up when I came back later. Who knew what stories other people were telling about your family, what trite tragedies they might be inventing without your permission? Your bedroom light was off, I saw. I imagined the white-noise whirl of the fan above your bed, the hallucinatory light of the aquarium wavering over your floor. The books that would be your only language now, and would your mother ever buy you more? Or would she now, permanently, bet against you?

I called your mother; she hung up on me. I called your sister at her dorm room; she swore into the phone. I called your mother; she told me she was calling the police. I drove by your house, this time less slowly, this time in the daytime, and stared up at your bedroom window. I couldn't tell if the lights were on. I saw your mother on the porch, holding a cell phone and shouting. I put my head down on the steering wheel, and waited for what would happen next.

Chapter 19

IT'S FALL IN HERE already, unbelievably. The Red Sox are headed to the World Series. Professional sports are an extremely expensive form of tribalist derangement, and I will not be induced to care about them now. But I will admit it buoys the spirit to have so many people around me rooting for the impossible. It's a metaphor for their own predicaments, naturally. Nevertheless.

I dream sometimes of jack-o'-lanterns. Ghoulishly amused, vibrating at some imperceptible frequency. Bouncing soundlessly down a hill.

Something that has struck me as interesting lately is how many people seem to think I am stupid. Deluded, pathetic, childlike, naïve, consumed with a perverse fantasy, incapable of registering the obvious. Something like a young girl becoming absolutely convinced that some celebrity is destined to love her—though much less endearing, of course, less explicable, less benign. Why I would develop such a fixation in the first place is partly explained, in this telling, by the fact of the dead husband: undone by grief, unhinged by loneliness, the poor idiot took solace in the only person she could find. She was broken enough to need her victim's love, dim enough to believe in it; her daffy technology gave her the means to write herself a whole romantic storyline without ever knowing she was doing it.

This is actually a relatively sympathetic interpretation of events. My lawyer is, I think, inclined to run with it as subtext; he could see early on that I really do believe what I'm saying. I would prefer he not drag Peter into it, but at this point, I am willing to make some concessions. An insanity defense is of course out of the question.

I am interested, however, in the subject of my stupidity. In my own defense, I'd like to make the case for the prosecution.

If I had to make myself the villain in our story, this is how I'd do it. I would begin not with my vulnerability but my arrogance.

I am born into a lower-middle-class family. My father dies while I am young, and I am raised alone by an idealistic mother. She works in the prisons and believes in anyone's redemption. I marry too young, have a baby too early. But I am also smart (a little less than I think I am) and ambitious (a little more than anyone around me realizes). The sheer stubbornness that gets me into Harvard also gets me kicked out of it; in between, I militantly adopt, then dramatically disavow, a bunch of obscure theories. These, in the view of my counsel, would not much interest the jury.

My husband dies.

(And how, exactly? Others, too, would like to know. He had a back injury; he had sleep apnea; he had pills. He left the kind of note he often did: some distant affection, some pragmatic reminders. He spends five days in a coma. "Does he know he's still alive?" I keep asking the doctors. "Hearing is the last to go," they say, irrelevantly. I hope to God he never knew. He would have hated all of it so much.)

Languages differentiate between causing and letting. And then there are the things no one ever talks about at all.

I suffer a miscarriage. I move back in with my mother. I will not fully admit that I've been kicked out of Harvard— an early sign of my capacity for denial. Subconsciously, I am looking for redemption. I do want to help people—I am not fundamentally motivated by malice, though this is irrelevant from a legal perspective and probably a moral one as well. I am also extremely afraid of boredom. I know that I am capable and, deep down, believe that I am special. I am intellectually flexible, but I don't yet know that about myself. I am also very lonely, but I don't know that yet either. I am a twenty-seven-year-old widow and have never really been in love.

In the midst of omnidirectional catastrophe, the Center offers me a lifeline. After a few months on the job, my entire intellectual framework is upended; within a year, I've abandoned the philosophical and linguistic theories that I once, with inappropriate ferocity, defended. I am also, it must be noted, not remotely a trained scientist. I am ultimately motivated by my own sense of meaning: I find it meaningful to believe that I am helping people, and so I do. My high verbal intelligence and superficial grasp of linguistic trivia help to obscure the fact—to myself and others—that I am making some extremely basic mistakes.

The first client I'm assigned to work with independently is a young man my own age—conventionally attractive, despite his many impairments. His mother believes fervently in his intellectual capacities; she is desperate to find the key that will unlock him, and return him to her once again. I believe that I might have that key. In this context, the Ouija-board-type communications typical of client sessions go further than they ever have before; I am thrilled by these early encounters, which begin to occupy a disproportionate space in my mental life. Slowly, unconsciously, I create for my interlocutor an entire personality, complete with jokes and opinions and interests that align strangely well with my own. If this person feels supernaturally familiar—supernaturally *correct*—this is because I am creating him. The dubious premise of the therapy—that I am the only person in the world who can speak to my beloved—only reinforces my romantic delusion. The notion that I am having a spectacular success in my professional life flatters my intellectual ego. I haven't been on a date since the death of my husband, and haven't had sex in almost two years. When I finally initiate a sexual encounter with my victim, I take his involuntary physical responses as signs of consent.

In my mind, we are the most fated and persecuted of lovers. But it is impossible to know what is in my victim's mind. In all our time together, he hasn't really said a word.

So yes, I know perfectly well how it looks. If I were peering in from the outside, I'd probably believe it myself. But here's a riddle I cannot answer, even after thinking about it for a good long while.

If I am capable of telling myself that story, then how could any of it be true?

Chapter 20

THE TRIAL—I WONDER IF you'd agree?—was both surreal and extremely dull: frightening in the way of Kafka's bureaucrats, or the sort of nightmare that contains large spiders as well as long stretches of fiddling with various doors and keys. The whole thing had the atemporal quality of an ancient ritual, with its baffling internal logic and meanings accrued through repetition. The fractured structure and meaningless redundancies tended to interrupt any sense of forward momentum. The verdict seemed simultaneously unknowable and preordained, like the answer to a question of arithmetic in a foreign number system, and I kept losing the thread of my own terror. Perhaps this is why I find myself remembering the trial not chronologically but categorically—sorting its events by their symbolic similarities, like a Japanese schoolchild, and recalling all of them in present tense.

The prosecution is a slick, potato-fed man, bred to look somewhat dumber than he actually is. His primary concern is establishing your nonexistence: an assertion reified by your absence from the courtroom itself. I have no idea if you would have wanted to come, though I'm certain no one has asked you. The advantage of this is that you're spared a parade of colorful pronouncements about the exact kind of void you are.

These come first from the experts, to cow everyone else into submission. One Dr. Julius A. Sargent has the integrity to note that your verbal impairments preclude confident evaluation of your intelligence; nevertheless, he is all too happy to share that on a standard IQ test, you score a 44. (*I'd like to know the standard IQ of anyone surprised by this, you might have said.*) The jurors write this figure down, obediently.

Your family is then called to make this number into a story, the sum of a subtraction. Moira takes the stand first. Her hair is slick with gel, yet somehow frizzier; the scar above her eyebrow arches when she frowns, which is often. Her task, it seems, is to speak of who you weren't—some other human, some other brother—and convey how much she'd suffered from this person's absence. Her testimony for some reason includes an anecdote about your having a sei-zure on the day of her seventh birthday party: you nearly died choking on apple sauce, and she never had any friends over again. One of the jurors, unbelievably, is crying.

Moira's witness account of the criminal act—which comes either much or only slightly later—is comparatively restrained. In the balcony, the media people visibly lean for-ward. They have been so inhumanly patient in their wait for this moment. But Moira reports on what she saw with dis-appointing efficiency—though in her tone one can hear her profound disgust with me, and you, and the alarming fact of sexual love more generally.

Your mother, on the other hand, is entirely unguarded. She weeps as she describes your disappearance, the profun-dity of her joy at your mirage-like reemergence. The dev-astating realization that it was all of it, all of it, a lie. This was so much worse than losing you the first time, she says through many sobs.

My lawyer—whose darting attempts at cross-examination have been tepidly deferential throughout—rouses himself here for some basic Socratic weaseling. Prior to the events of March 25, he asks, did your mother believe you had the full intellectual capacities of a man of twenty-eight?

She admits that she did.

And did she find it unusual that a man of twenty-eight might wish to embark on a consensual romantic relationship?

She admits she did not.

And yet, as soon as she had learned that her own son had done so, her entire understanding of his cognition suddenly had changed—was that correct?

Your mother concedes that this is so.

"And why was that?" my lawyer asks her.

"I wanted so badly to believe it," your mother says, and I wonder if she's aware of echoing Moira precisely. "But when I found out what she was doing with my son"—the record is amended to reflect that your mother is gesturing toward the defendant—"I realized *she* must have wanted to believe it, too." Your mother bows her head. "And then the whole thing fell apart."

In my memory, your mother's statement is followed by a sort of pause for intermission, compounding its dramatic impact.

At some point they bring in Tyruil, that old shit. He offers up a breathless account of the encounter on the T, although, for the most part, I decline to listen. I don't want that man's nasal voice hovering above my own memories of that day. How my hair curtained your face, falling in a way that might have happened any time by accident but had also happened other times, for other reasons. The sting of spotting Tyruil's obnoxious face across the platform, amidst the whirl of transport. The sudden knowledge that our movements must have implied those other movements, made them briefly visible in silhouette or shadow. The way I dropped your elbow; the way, a heartbeat earlier, I had held it. The close-call feeling of this moment, in the moment: an exhilaration that seemed to follow us out onto the water. How I felt it as I stood beside you later, watching that white-backed creature crest upon the ocean, tasting the fermented salt upon my lip. How it persisted no matter how many times I tongued it off.

My lawyer makes a whole big point of challenging Tyruil about this episode, making him enumerate all the many things he did not see that day. "Was my client kissing Mr. O'Keefe? Was she touching Mr. O'Keefe inappropriately? Did Mr. O'Keefe appear in any way distressed?" Tyruil answers "no" to all these questions until the judge gets bored. I wonder if part of the point of this litany is the repetition of the honorific "Mr."—if the lawyer is trying to reenforce your status as an adult by offering you the same basic courtesy as a newspaper style guide—though since no one ever called you this in real life, it all feels like a kind of perjury.

"And yet you still felt that something—inappropriate was going on?" the other lawyer asks Tyruil. There is an objection to this, which is sustained. Tyruil then, using his own words, clarifies that he felt *concerned* that something inappropriate was going on. It is entirely clear that he's having the time of his life. You can tell he's already figured out where he'll put all this on his CV.

"And what made you feel concerned?" the lawyer asks.

Here, Tyruil looks at me directly. He seems to be smirking, just a little. "Sometimes you just know," he says.

My lawyer again objects to this, naturally. But here, of course, I think Tyruil is right.

Tyruil's other area of expertise, unbelievably, concerns my state of mind. What I did or did not believe about what I was doing, which is another way of asking what I believed about what you were capable of understanding, specifically vis-à-vis the question of consent. My state of mind! Tyruil! Of all people! Tyruil, who has never given serious thought to any state of mind not his own. Incredibly, he has brought documentation: my own early papers. He quotes me arguing this, averring that. One senses he wishes desperately he could hold some kind of special pencil.

I hope he's condemned to some purgatory where it's only his own voice in his head—his own voice at its youngest, and dumbest, and wrongest. I hope this is the last voice he hears, and it echoes within him for eternity.

And somewhere in the midst of all of this, the grand finale: you are wheeled into the courtroom. A prosecutor's witness, of course. *A prop*, you would have said, correctly. I haven't seen you since the day they found us, the day I left you at your mother's table. You look paler than you did then, somehow diminished; you might have stood, of course, but don't. They've dressed you in yellow—emphatically not your color—a color for a toddler or an Easter egg, not an adult man in command of his own wits. *I'll see you soon*, I had said the last time that I saw you. I wonder if you'd known it wasn't true. In court, I try to catch your eye to ask, but they have you angled strategically away from me. The big advantage here, my lawyer tells me, is that no one can accuse you of being coached.

The device is wheeled in, enshrouded in a special cloth, and unveiled with some theater at the last moment. You can tell they wish they could have done something similar with you. The missing key, I see, has not been replaced; there's a sticky-looking stain on one side, positioned to be visible to the jury. A court-appointed physician sits beside you, while someone who seems to be the prosecutor's intern launches into a set of stupid questions. Your hand hangs limply within the physician's, who doesn't at all know what she's doing.

"Who is the president?" the intern asks.

And: "Do you know where you are today?"

And: "Can you tell us about your relationship with the defendant?"

It is occurring to me that this, all of this, is something like your worst nightmare. Did that ever occur to Moira? That she is putting you through the exact kind of public spectacle she'd accused me of plotting? The lights, the gallery of reporters. Me, your silently weeping mother. The array of medical experts blithely declaring you a vegetable. The gawking jury box, sequestered half the summer, nearly out of their minds with the need for a shocking catharsis.

"What is your sister's name?" the intern asks. "What street do you live on? Would you describe your romantic relationship with the defendant as consensual?"

We must imagine Sisyphus happy, I'd said to you once— probably in reference to a life in academia. *We must imagine Camus happy*, you said, and I laughed, although I did not entirely understand what you meant by this.

They ask questions until the only real question left is how long they'll let this all go on. At some point, they decide it's over, which forces my own lawyer to deliver the real indictment. He rises, shakes his head, and says, "No further questions."

On the way out, you do look at me—flashing me one of your intent, urgent looks, like that very first one that made me really see you. A flare shot out into the darkness, an SOS written on the sand. I hadn't known everything that first look meant, and I didn't know everything this one meant, either. But I know what I feared: that it meant you were saying goodbye.

I have been returning once again to the question of conceptual semantics: this idea that our minds come programmed with some basics, attuned to space and substance, agency and causation. Like a compass that can only point in four cardinal directions, until language fills in all the other points in the sphere.

This theory has the vote of the prelinguistic infant— sensitive already to cause and effect, agency and spatial relations. A normal person might wonder if there's anything else we come in with. Could there be a hardwired capacity for love? This is not a question philosophers or linguists would care to study. It is hideously sentimental, for one thing, yet somehow too academic for the academics. We cannot know, and it is embarrassing to speculate, and anyway, it does not matter.

In most lives, of course, it does not matter.

In optimistic moods, I remind myself that you did it all before. You endured a third of a life sentence, spent decades digging a tunnel with a spoon. You did it before, you can do it again. You know it is possible, now.

But another part of me knows that this time, they will not let you. And sometimes I think this is the only real use of my freedom: not that we might reunite, but that they might reconsider. Because if I'm convicted, they will never, ever change their minds. I will need to be a monster, you will need to be a thing, and they will need to believe all of this forever.

Because if they're wrong—oh God, if they're wrong— then what have they done?

Eventually I am called to the witness stand, where I try, against my lawyer's better judgment, to explain myself. I can tell my story is unsatisfying to both lawyers, in different ways. One senses they'd both like me gone, so they can explain the real story more clearly.

The questions are mercifully insipid: even the most prurient inquiries are too unimaginative to feel truly intrusive. Yes, some of the constituent aspects of our sexual relationship were awkward to consider abstractly—the device being the least of these when you really thought about it, which, in the moment, we did not. Yes, there were certain things you could do in bed that surprised me. It is true there were other things we could not do, but our attention was not on those things. You really have to wonder about people who ask questions like these.

From the jury, there's a palpable sense of disappointment. They expected me to be a certain shocking thing—or possibly, even more shockingly, the exact opposite of that. Finding themselves more or less un-scandalized, they now seem a little bored.

This probably doesn't help with their attention to the science. To speak in defense of the technology, my lawyer summons Pauline, promoted since Leana's departure. She has an incongruously lovely voice, Pauline, full of gentleness and light laughter; I remember how she put our clients at ease with that voice, and I hope she might have a similar effect on the jury. As far as I can tell, she's plucked the wart hair, though this I find depressing—the fact that she knew about it all along, and that *this* is the occasion that finally roused her intervention. I listen as she describes the triumphs of the Center—the Girl Who Wrote Poems, the Boy Who Spelled "Hope" (*Isn't that the title of Bill Clinton's autobiography?* I remember you'd said once)—and attests to my professionalism and skill during my time there. She offers approving remarks about my early success with you, though she admits she can't speak to the quality of my work after my official affiliation with the Center ended. Leana's problems come up, of course: the prosecutor reads at length from the *Globe* article in a breathy, strangely inflected cadence; I get the distinct impression he was an undergraduate poet. Pauline tries to cast the whole thing as a story of academic pettiness—a bunch of pointy-headed nihilists obsessed with trying to discredit anything that might be useful in the real world—which anyway, she stresses, has nothing to do with me. I'm not sure how this is landing. The prosecutor, I feel very certain, will pursue an MFA if no one stops him.

At some point, we revisit the issue of my character. Speaking on my behalf is my mother—though I'm told this will not count for much—and poor old Alan, like a sport. I am ashamed I was not kinder to him, ashamed it seems I didn't need to be. Both my mother and Alan refer to me—many times—as a "young mother," and significantly overstate the extent of JoJo's likely devastation should I be sentenced to a lengthy term in jail.

A language, as they say, is just a dialect with an army. It's occurring to me, too late, that these people were mine.

Your mother came to see me once, before the trial. Did she ever tell you that? A stupid question: I doubt she tells you anything anymore.

I'd put her on my visitor list in the ludicrous hope that she might somehow bring you along to see me. Nevertheless,

I was extremely surprised when she showed up. We sat together on a bench in the scrubby yard outside the jail. She
was wearing overalls and turquoise glasses I'd never seen before. She kept blinking through them hard, as though the
light was bothering her.

"I didn't know you needed glasses," I said.

"They tell me that I do."

"I like them."

"Good," your mother said. "I only came here to ask."

I laughed to let her know I understood I was ridiculous.

Your mother bunched her hair atop her head, seemed
to realize she had nothing to tie it with, then let it fall back
down again.

"I had an uncle in prison once," she said.

"Me too," I said. "He was a meth dealer in Nevada. What
was your guy in for?"

"Same thing." She was jackrabbiting her leg already,
though she must have had a cigarette in the car. "Though it
wasn't meth. Or Nevada." She barked a weird little laugh I
hadn't heard before. "You're just full of surprises, aren't you?
I always thought your family was fancy."

I shrugged.

"You know I didn't even know you had a kid?" she said.
"I had to read about it in the papers."

"Yes, you did." I'd told her that night on your porch—
about Josephine, about her bald spot. I was surprised she
didn't remember, surprised that this could still hurt me.

"You literally never talked about her," she said.

"I was trying to be professional."

"Is that supposed to be a joke?"

There was obviously no right answer to this.

"You actually worked for *us*, you know?" your mother said. "Isn't that so funny? I mean, isn't that so strange? Here you were, swooping around with your technology and your Harvard PhD and your thousand-dollar words. And all your theories!" She honked that new laugh of hers again. "I was so scared of you, you know? Even before you were fucking my son. I was fucking *scared* of you."

Hers was a grief cut with shame, I recognized abruptly. An awareness that people would always have their questions, that their sympathy would come spiked with skepticism. When Peter died, people did not know what to say; they spoke as though the darker possibility might never have occurred to us. *And if they don't know*—the thinking seemed to be—*let's never tell them. (And if they don't know, what else might they have missed?)* We were treated like cursed children, incapable of understanding either what we had done or what we had endured. *(And if their innocence could be this dangerous, who knew what they'd do with any real knowledge?)*

"I'm sorry," I said. I wanted to tell her she hadn't needed to be scared of me. But I knew she'd only say she hadn't been nearly scared enough.

"And all that time, I was actually your *employer*. Moira had to remind me of that! You were my employee, and all I ever had to do was fire you."

"But why would you have done that?" I said. "You were really happy with his progress."

"Who gives a shit if I was happy? I was happy when he

was a toddler, too. What actually matters is what comes next."

I thought of your mother on that first day I met you, the day she showed me your baby pictures. I remembered the way she'd scoured them, looking for the exact place you'd disappeared. She was ready to dive in after you, I knew, just as soon as she found the spot to try. I suppose that turned out to be me, in the end, no matter how you look at things.

"Well, if it makes you feel any better," I said, "I don't actually have a PhD."

Your mother made a sound that was either a cough or the new laugh.

Hopefully, I added, "And we really *were* going to tell you."

But this, evidently, was the wrong thing: your mother was looking at me with real concern now—an expression that felt nearly parental. She leaned toward me, and I caught a whiff of old smoke and dishwashing soap and knock-off pharmacy perfume.

"Do you really still think that's the point?" she said.

I shook my head. I wished, with a strange little upsurge of emotion, that I could embrace her then—so that I could study her scent in more detail, so that I could, just maybe, find you within it. I remembered how she'd done this to you, on the occasion of the Serious Conversation. I remembered how she'd breathed you in—trying one last time to know you on her own terms, in one of the only ways she ever could. I suppose you could call this a kind of skepticism. At the time, it seemed to me a sort of faith.

The light across the grass rippled strangely, and I looked up to see a flock of geese go by.

I said: "I saw old Badger Dick at the hearing."

Your mother laugh-grimaced, then tried to iron out her face.

"I told the lawyers he has nothing at all to do with Sammy. But I guess that doesn't matter. He's allowed to be there, apparently." She made that backward full-body eye roll I remembered from the first day I met her. "He'll probably use the whole thing to promote his Tandromat."

"His *what?*"

She sliced her eyes in my direction without actually rotating her head. I wondered if she'd gotten that move from you, or the other way around.

"It's tanning while you do your laundry." She exhaled some phantom nicotine. "It's fully coin operated."

"But where are your supposed to keep your quarters?"

Your mother gave a smirk, very nearly a smile, and I could feel it touch that stupid thing within me that hopes its stupid hopes. Like a vestigial organ that's useless at its very best and explodes when it gets too worked up.

"You know what's really fucked up?" she said. "I actually kind of miss you sometimes."

"I miss you too!" I said. "God, I miss all of you so much."

"Well, that's good," she said. The smirk was gone now—or had I imagined it entirely? On her face was a new expression—something sour and real, too quotidian to have its own noun. "I mean, you're probably gonna have to get used to missing people."

I felt a tubercular thickening in my throat then. I might have cried, harnessing sentiment to strategy, but I decided I would not. I could feel your mother sense this impulse and its suppression; I somehow knew that she respected it.

"Sandi, can I tell you what really scares me?" I said. I was whispering now, I realized. "I'm just so worried you might be wrong. I mean, what if you're *wrong*? And if you are, then we're leaving him all alone. Bored. Depressed. Probably terrified." Though this I didn't entirely believe. "And I know you're still working things out in your mind—"

"I'm not," your mother said, matter-of-factly. "This is why you're *incarcerated*, if you haven't noticed."

Then why are you here? I would have asked if I wasn't so afraid the asking would make her go away again. But clearly the question had posed itself: your mother stood and began gathering her things, waiting until what seemed like the very last second to hand me a manila envelope.

"But I did bring you this," she said. "It's that fucking essay. We found it when we were cleaning out his room."

I stared at the envelope, my own name written neatly upon it.

"This was only the outline," I said. The space behind my eyes felt drained, as though I'd cried backward, or somehow metaphorically. "What were you cleaning out his room for?"

"Moira didn't want me to bring it," your mother said. "But I figured, hey, either way, it's yours, right? I mean, after all, you wrote it."

"I only typed it." My hands, I saw, were shaking slightly. "Sandi, are you sending him away somewhere?"

"You know I had to look up who Chekhov was?" Your mother snorted. "I felt like such a dumbass. And here I'd somehow raised a *genius* without even trying."

"You raised two," I said. Though it galled me, still, to say this. "I mean, Moira's pretty smart and all."

"She's a whole lot sharper than I am, that's for sure."

"Sandi, please don't send him anywhere."

"Don't make me sorry I came," your mother said. "Sometimes a person cleans a room, all right? And believe it or not, I am no longer seeking your professional opinion."

"OK," I said. I stared again at the envelope. Really, it was only notes, and I knew even then that it couldn't be why she'd come. I'd understand the real reason only later, when I opened the envelope and three photographs fell out. They were of the three of us at Christmas—you and your elf hat, your mother with her earrings, me in the distressingly pale half-deranged face I hope I make only in photographs. Your image, frankly, is upsetting. A clearly disabled person in an elf hat might look whimsical were it not for that atrocious sweater; you'd worn it as a joke, but in the picture you don't look like the sort of person who can afford to make jokes at his own expense. It seems instead as though someone else has dressed you—probably cruelly—probably that sheet-white banshee beside you whose intentions can only be malign. (There's an entire one-act play in that photo. I am eternally grateful it did not show up in court.) Your mother, however, is radiant, staring straight into the camera as she holds it above us, so joy limned you would think that she's the one in love. She lights up the whole room, your mother, including those two ghouls beside her.

It had been the greatest season of her life too, I realized, while looking at those pictures. Your reemergence had been her dream and happiest passion, and now she couldn't even regard it as a memory. Instead, she'd managed to convince herself it had all been a delusion or worse; she had forced herself to believe your resurrection had never happened, and yet somehow, by not happening, she had annihilated the possibility it ever might. And yet here I was, still living in the world where you were real—free to live there forever, even if I spent the rest of my life locked up. Your mother couldn't visit that place anymore. But she still liked to imagine it. And that, I realized, is why she'd come to see me: so that I might tell her a story. It was a story she wanted to remember, and she needed to hear it one last time.

"I do love him," I told her after a while.

And after another whole long while, she said, "I know."

Chapter 21

I HAVE BEEN THINKING lately about memory. It has been argued that thoughts store memories in ways more abstract than sentences. Our words are Flaubert's cracked instruments for bears to dance to; it's our inner lives that hold the music that they hear.

This doesn't solve the mystery of which way the circuit runs, of course. But it's intuitively appealing and, for me, consoling to imagine our early words this way—as the fragmentary hieroglyphs of a vast civilization we were together uncovering.

A life of the mind is still highly possible in here. They let me have books, pencils, everything I need to continue my work. I sit in my cell and read and write and study, and I never go out and eat dreadfully, and it's not so different, in the end, from preparing a dissertation.

"The Navajo have something like a dozen words for 'eat,'" I tell the jailer who brings me my meals. "Depending on what is being consumed." I poke at the gray gristly hide of my hamburger. There is a way to request vegetarian food in here, but I know how to pick my battles.

"If I could give you one piece of advice, it would be to keep your mouth shut," she says. "If you were half as smart as you think you are, then you wouldn't be here at all."

And with this, she closes the door behind her.

*

I've been revisiting *Pale Fire* lately, though I can't quite make my theory line up again. Something had converged in just the right way to let me see something new: ignorance colliding with fractional knowledge to create a different lens. For a moment, I thought I understood religion, or why people get their PhDs in English. Because if Botkin was a deluded conspiracy-minded academic, then that meant I was too! This felt like a resolution of its own sort: the puzzle jumping off the page and making me a part of it, uniting the viewer with the viewed.

I'm still hacking away at the Russian. I am appalled by the terrifyingly innumerate ways a word can end.

On the second day of deliberations, my mother comes to see me.

She brings along a picture of Josephine, who looks ruddier now, her hair nice and robust. "She's growing up," I say, although I'm not sure that's what's happening at all.

There are the ritual inquiries and lamentations, and then my mother says: "I have some news." She ducks her head; for the first time in her entire life, she looks nearly shy. "Alan and I are getting married."

There is hooting and amazement up and down the hall; the Red Sox, unbelievably, have won the World Series.

"You crazy kids!" I say, and kiss her. "How wonderful."

"Well, we've been talking about it for a while." And there

it is: a once-in-a-lifetime blush. I am very glad to be there to see it. "And we just thought now, with Josephine—well, we just thought it would be good to have the both of us around."

"Oh," I say. "Of course." Although I hadn't thought of that. I look down at Josephine's picture; though her hair looks good, she is making a pretty dopey expression, baring her teeth in an overbite she doesn't really have.

"But I really might be coming home, you know," I say.

"Well of *course* you're coming home." My mother sounds a little savage; this is not a tone she would have ever taken with a client. I look back down at Josephine. I wonder if she is copying someone with that cartoon-rabbit expression—if she knows somebody with a bucktooth grin like that, and if she likes them. I wonder if she's glad she'll have a real grandfather now, or if she is the kind of little girl who likes a wedding.

"Oh, we didn't bother with all that," my mother says. She means a ring, I guess—she must think I'd been looking at her hands.

"No," I say, and look back up at her. "Well, that isn't the part that matters."

My mother taps on Josephine's picture—a little sadly, I think. "Those teeth," she says. And then: "You used to be so good with her."

There's a toneless shriek from somewhere down the hall—residual sports hysteria, or the start of one of the more typical disasters, I can't tell.

"Was I?" I say. "I don't remember."

And neither will Josephine, it goes without saying.

"Sometimes I think I took over for you too much," my mother says. "When Peter died."

"I don't want to talk about Peter."

"I know," she says, and sighs. "And I indulged that, too."

I look at my mother's hands. They are wafery now, the color of oatmeal. It occurs to me, very dimly, that she will die one day.

"I know you like to blame yourself for everything," I say. "But I'm not going to let you take credit for this one. Because when I think about my life. I mean. When I think about my *life*—this is the only thing I'm very sure was meant to happen."

"You're getting pretty mystical in here."

"That belief is *not* mystical," I say. "It's evidential. It is derived from my direct perception and experience."

"I guess I have to take your word for that."

"Oh, *would* you?"

I am crying again, I realize.

"I said I *have* to," my mother says. "So I wouldn't get too grateful."

We are holding hands somehow. We stay like that a while.

"I mean, I do *have* to," she says. "Don't I?"

The Kawésqar of Chile have one past tense for the literal and another for the mythical. Sometimes it seems the real question before the jury is which one should be used to tell our story.

*

Josephine, it has been decided, should not visit during the trial.

This way, she might not have to remember me here at all, my mother says—and though I do not like this strategy, who am I to say she's wrong? There are limits on what you can reasonably ask from a child. I've bumped up against a few of them myself, over the years.

They tell Josephine I'm in a timeout for a while.

"But *why* are you in a timeout?" she asks the fourth time I call her.

I've thought a lot about how to answer this question.

"I'm in a timeout because I broke the rules," I say, and I can almost hear her nodding sagely.

"Like the time I ate those mice," she says.

"No, sweetheart," I say, and clench the phone. "I broke the rules that time, too."

"So which rule did you break?" my daughter asks the next time. She's a pro at accepting collect calls by now.

I lower my voice for this one; I don't want anyone here to hear me. They all know, of course, and some of them act like I'm a child molester. But most of them just find the whole thing extremely funny, which is in some ways worse.

"I fell in love with someone I should not have," I tell my daughter.

"Oh," she says, sounding knowing. She has apparently become quite attached to the school librarian—a very sweet, very obviously gay young man, who has given her a whole pile of those awful Boxcar books, the ones where one child's entire personality is that he's always hungry and another's is that she's always weeping. So perhaps JoJo felt she understood—my tender, my uncomplicated child.

"So did you have *sex* with him?" she asks.

"Josephine!"

"What?" she says. Her voice trills with subversion. She knows about sex, of course—it's part of my mother's healthy-minded pragmatism to explain such things quite early—but I am certain she has zero awareness of, and even less curiosity about, its more slippery social aspects. Still, I find the question unnerving.

"That is absolutely none of your business," I say.

She huffs in a way that reminds me of my mother and says, "I think maybe it is."

"Good *lord*," I say. "Just what on earth is your grandmother telling you?"

"Nothing," my daughter says, and now she sounds a little bratty. "That's the whole point. She always says I'll understand things when I'm older, or that she'll explain stuff later. But now I just think she's lying."

"I don't think she's *lying*," I say. Josephine issues an uptalk-inflected grunt, the tone of some wordless rebuttal: *How would you know?* Or maybe: *Why should I believe you?*

In the background, I can hear my mother shouting out an answer at *Jeopardy!*. I wish I knew the question.

"I think there are some things you probably won't ever understand," I say to my daughter. "But I promise to keep trying to explain them."

*

According to Barthes, myth is neither a truth nor a confession: it is an inflexion.

*

There is one last thing I never told you, and it doesn't reflect well on me at all.

I am thinking of that day in March, when Moira was home, and we were so newly in love, and your mother made what would, I suppose, be her final attempt to speak with you. I can't imagine it's any secret that I did not think this conversation would work. All that nervous formality, the intensity of the stakes. Your sister radiating her aggrieved skepticism. Your mother's inability to drop her aura of *performance*; the loudly symbolic way she wore those earrings you had given her at Christmas. And of course she wasn't holding your arm right.

And so, when we failed, I was not surprised. But a tiny, poisonous part of me was glad.

I caught this hideousness in an instant. I was glad you couldn't talk to your mother because it appealed to my sense of *romance?* This was your life we were talking about. There's a pathologic possessiveness to early love, yes—*you are mine*, something within must have hissed: *mine truly and mine only*—but this, I knew even then, was no loving form for it to take. And for a long time, I wondered if that single moment meant I didn't deserve to love you, or be loved by you, at all.

But I never let you weigh in on this question, and I guess that isn't great. A superstitious person might believe I'm being punished for that.

It is true I always believed I could make it up to you. That if I didn't quite merit your love, there was still, would always be, a bit more time to earn it. A foolishness that, I'm pretty sure, is universal. Perhaps we can never make ourselves worthy of certain graces. Perhaps we can still deserve to keep trying.

*

On the tenth night of deliberations, my daughter asks: "Did he love you too?"

"Yes," I say.

"Did he tell you that?"

I think for a moment and say, "I think so." And then I pretend my time is up, so I can cry the way I want to.

You live inside me now, of course—your mind, your circuitry, your soundless voice. And yes, I expect that I similarly inhabit you. But that isn't the consolation one might think; in fact, it's the entire problem. Anything less, and we wouldn't be here at all.

I often think about your grand saga, of the fortune teller and the illusionist. I know you were kind of joking about it all. Still, sometimes I wonder if you knew where it was going. I wonder if you knew how it ended. Sometimes I make up endings of my own.

This could become a hobby, I suppose, in case I ever find myself in need of one.

"Man does not exist prior to language, either as a species or as an individual." That's Barthes again. I consider it the blessing of my life that I will never again be so sure of anything.

At night, I think of the hieroglyphs, of our joint civilization. The linguistic determinists would say we were not uncovering it but building it. That you did not really exist until we created you, together.

I know profoundly that this isn't true.

I also know that if it were, I would not be sorry.

Unrepentant, I await your verdict.

Acknowledgments

Endless thanks to my readers for their insight and encouragement: Dalia Azim, Lydia Conklin, Emma Copley Eisenberg, Hillery Hugg, Adam Krause, Chris Leslie-Hynan, Jill Meyers, Becka Oliver, Maya Perez, Mary Helen Specht, and Tony Tulathimutte.

Thanks to my agent, Henry Dunow, and my editor, Daniel Slager. Thanks to the entire team at Milkweed, including Yanna Demkiewicz, Morgan LaRocca, Lauren Langston Klein, and Mary Austin Speaker.

Thanks to Roman Butvin, for the Chekhov insight; John Greenman, for the legal perspective; and Guy Deutscher, John McWhorter, and Steven Pinker, for the thinking about language.

Thanks to my Texas State graduate students for making me believe in fiction over and over and over again.

And thanks most of all to Justin, Theo, and Milo, who are the joy and meaning of my life.

Justin Perry

JENNIFER DUBOIS's debut novel, *A Partial History of Lost Causes*, was the winner of the California Book Award for First Fiction, the Northern California Book Award for Fiction, a Whiting Award, a National Book Foundation 5 Under 35 Award, and was a finalist for the PEN/ Hemingway Award for Debut Fiction. Her second novel, *Cartwheel*, was a finalist for the New York Public Library's Young Lions Award and the winner of the Housatonic Book Award. DuBois's third novel, *The Spectators*, was a recipient of a National Endowment for the Arts Creative Writing Fellowship and a Civitella Ranieri Fellowship. A graduate of the Iowa Writers' Workshop and the Stanford University Stegner Fellowship, duBois teaches in the MFA program at Texas State University. *The Last Language* is her fourth novel.

milkweed
EDITIONS

Founded as a nonprofit organization in 1980,
Milkweed Editions is an independent publisher. Our
mission is to identify, nurture, and publish transformative
literature, and build an engaged community around it.

Milkweed Editions is based in Bdé Óta Othúŋwe
(Minneapolis) within Mní Sota Makhóčhe, the traditional
homeland of the Dakhóta people. Residing here since
time immemorial, Dakhóta people still call Mní Sota
Makhóčhe home, with four federally recognized Dakhóta
nations and many more Dakhóta people residing in what
is now the state of Minnesota. Due to continued legacies
of colonization, genocide, and forced removal, generations
of Dakhóta people remain disenfranchised from their
traditional homeland. Presently, Mní Sota Makhóčhe has
become a refuge and home for many Indigenous nations
and peoples, including seven federally recognized Ojibwe
nations. We humbly encourage our readers to reflect upon
the historical legacies held in the lands they occupy.

milkweed.org

Milkweed Editions, an independent nonprofit publisher, gratefully acknowledges sustaining support from our Board of Directors; the Alan B. Slifka Foundation and its president, Riva Ariella Ritvo-Slifka; the Amazon Literary Partnership; the Ballard Spahr Foundation; *Copper Nickel*; the McKnight Foundation; the National Endowment for the Arts; the National Poetry Series; and other generous contributions from foundations, corporations, and individuals. Also, this activity is made possible by the voters of Minnesota through a Minnesota State Arts Board Operating Support grant, thanks to a legislative appropriation from the arts and cultural heritage fund. For a full listing of Milkweed Editions supporters, please visit milkweed.org.

  NATIONAL ENDOWMENT for the ARTS arts.gov   MᶜKNIGHT FOUNDATION

Interior design by Mary Austin Speaker
Typeset in Adobe Jenson Pro

Adobe Jenson was designed by Robert Slimbach for Adobe
and released in 1996. Slimbach based Jenson's roman styles
on a text face cut by fifteenth-century type designer
Nicolas Jenson, and its italics are based on type created
by Ludovico Vicentino degli Arrighi, a late fifteenth-
century papal scribe and type designer.